Also by Benjamin Roberts:

The Girl I Knew

https://www.amazon.co.uk/Girl-I-Knew-Benjamin-Roberts/dp/0993012809

For Andrew,

Benjamin Roberts.

THE MOONDISH
月亮菜

Benjamin Roberts

For Georgiana Barrowcliff

and

Jenny Hancock

"Here there was laughing of old, there was weeping,
Haply, of lovers none ever will know,
Whose eyes went seaward a hundred sleeping
Years ago."

Algernon Swinburne *The Forsaken Garden* 1876

Moon (mūn), sb 1. The satellite of the earth; a secondary planet, whose light, derived from the sun, is reflected to the earth, and serves to dispel the darkness of the night. b. Since the disappearance of O.E. grammatical genders, the moon has been treated as feminine; in poetry it is sometimes, after classical example, identified with various goddesses.

Moo-nbeam. 1590. A ray of moonlight.

Moo-nblind; Moo-nblink, a temporary evening blindness caused by sleeping in the moonshine in tropical climates 1830. Hence **Moon-blindness.**

Moo-n-calf A mooning, absent-minded person. 1613.

Moondial 1686. A dial for showing the hours of the night by the moon.

Moondish. [1850. Rose Olivia Cotton, 'The Magic of the Undercliff'] (unexpl.) The apex of the reflection of moonlight on the sea, appar.   in conjunction with a requisite predisposition of young sexual longing confers abilities upon the viewer which are occult in nature.

PROLOGUE

1849

The Speaking

Captain Aloysius Pendleton rolls over in his bed in the main house aft. He scratches his beard, thick with salt, stretches his arms, listens to the creak of the rigging, feeling the run of the ship. He knows that all is still just about well before he hears the strike of the bell, two, two and one. Five bells, half past six in the morning. Soon the steward will bring breakfast and he will take over from the first mate and head the ship, well South of Hainan and just North of the Paracel Islands, towards Hong Kong harbour, only two days away, God willing, if the South West breeze holds steady. He lowers his arms to curb a strong waft of his acrid bodily stench. He needs a wash, he knows, but the fresh water supply is low and there has been no rain for weeks. Besides, the crew are just the same. They all stink. And they are a miserable lot since the storm. Rations are low and Huggins the Carpenter had gone overboard two days ago. Pendleton is desperate to reach Hong Kong harbour, and prays that he won't meet any pirate junks on the way.

"Sail ho!" A yell from the Watch on the deck above, repeated, "Sail ho!"

Pendleton reaches for his breeches and pea jacket, grabs his telescope and wrenches back the door, colliding with the steward, knocking the small tray of fried salted beef, potatoes and coffee all over the deck.

"Where away?" He yells. He has to lift his feet over the head of the steward who is on his knees, clawing up the food and stuffing it into his mouth.

Pendleton is feeling a sharp pain of hunger as he reaches the aft deck. Was there any coffee left? Any water left?

"Starboard bow, Captain." The mate is holding his brass telescope fully extended, "A three master. Barque. No," He squints and murmurs, "She's a Clipper. Making slow against the headwind."

"We'll try to speak her, then. Pray bring the trumpet and the blackboard." Pendleton raises his heavy telescope. "Alter course. Six degrees to the North-East."

"Six points North-East." The mate shouts aft to the helmsman at the wheel.

As the helm complies and his ship slowly turns her length and wide girth to the new course, Pendleton can just make out the glitter of gold lettering under the bow of the approaching vessel. She is reefed down against the breeze, topgallants and topsails stowed, making slow progress against the wind which gives Pendleton, going the other way, a fair speed. The name is "Sea Witch".

Pendleton runs his glass down her lines. She could easily have out-run him on the same tack, he thinks. As she draws closer, he can see the Captain clearly, bent over a black board, carefully inscribing his message in chalk. Two deckhands then raise the blackboard up on the rail and the lettering is clear through Pendleton's glass. "*ENGLISH CLIPPER SEA WITCH 2 DAYS FROM HONG KONG BOUND FOR LONDON. CAPTAIN EDWIN DOE REQUESTS TRANSFER OF PASSENGER.*"

Pendleton is curious, then alarmed. The Sea Witch isn't a real clipper, she is too small. And what was wrong? Why would they want to transfer a passenger only two days out? Illness? He certainly doesn't wish for a passenger who may be sick. He has no doctor. His medicine chest is rudimentary. True, there is a small hospital in Hong Kong but that is two days away, even with a following wind. It might be contagious. He scans the decks of the Sea Witch, now only two cables away, noting the clean gleam of the decks, the shining brass, the well-dressed crew, the order. He can see nothing wrong or untoward. He notices two officers amidships, legs wide apart as they stand against the roll of the deck, one gripping a bottle of champagne, carefully helping themselves into two cut-glass tumblers. Pendleton turns to the first mate, "Stand by with the launch. Write out the following. Please clarify intention and identify proposed transferee and reason for transfer."

The mate takes the chalk and slowly inscribes the words, each letter slanted by the roll of his body. Two of the crew hold the blackboard up. Three others are busy uncovering the stiff canvas from the launch.

After a few minutes, Pendleton can see Captain Doe quickly chalking. But then his telescope catches another movement. A dark figure appears from the cabin of the afterhouse behind the main mast and stands motionless. He focusses, the telescope yawing in his grip. A woman. She seems to be wearing a veil, holding it down against her face in the wind, the folds of her black gown moving slightly. Even at this distance, and regardless of the veil covering her head, Pendleton can feel her gaze. She is looking directly at him.

The blackboard on the Sea Witch is raised up on the rail again. This time, closer, Pendleton can read the words without his glass, "INTENTION RETURN HONG KONG, TRANSFER MISS ALICE CAPPER, MISSIONARY. INDISPOSED."

Pendleton lowers his glass. He doesn't want a woman on board. He doesn't want an ill woman on board and he doesn't want a sick female missionary on board. He raises his glass again across the shortening span and with a tiny twist of the lens focusses in on the black figure. As if acknowledging his inspection, she leans against the woodwork, slowly raises her veil and shows her face. Pendleton feels her challenge even at this distance, his fingers shaking, turning the lens to sharpen the image. She is horribly disfigured. Her hands are held together in prayer as she looks at him, mouthing words he cannot hear.

With a slow outbreath, Pendleton gently lays down the scope on the binnacle, turns to the mate and grunts. "Make an excuse. We have no medicine, no doctor. Anything else you can think of," He turns to the door of the gangway, "And resume course as before."

The girl's face, his disquiet and his Christian conscience stays with Pendleton until he has finally finished a much depleted breakfast, a few pieces of dry bread and soupy coffee made with water that tastes of tin. Then the reason for his unease dawns on him. Edwin Doe's word *Clipper,* the beautiful lines of the Sea Witch, her immaculate condition, her well-dressed crew, the champagne. Only one cargo would pay for all that in 1849. Aloysius Pendleton nods his head and reaches for his Bible. He was well to stay clear. The Sea Witch was a so-called tea clipper, but smaller, faster. Hereabouts everyone knows that means an opium runner.

And there was something else. Something else about the ship which had disturbed him. Pendleton must have noticed it only subconsciously, but now he remembered. The face of the figurehead at its prow. That face was the face of the girl, Alice Capper, disfigured missionary.

PART ONE

Jane Tench

1

I put the photocopied hand-written sheet down.

"No. Never seen anything like it." I shook my head and smiled, "1849? South China Sea? I'm a narrative therapist, not a literary critic." I let the smile drop, "Nor a historian."

"Me neither, Miss Tench. I've never seen anything like it either in 40 years of being a psychotherapist. The young man who wrote it, Adam Doe, is in a bad way, suicidal I would say Miss Tench." The consultant Driscoll lowered his spectacles on his bulky nose and peered out of the Isle of Wight NHS window overlooking Newport Harbour, boats left tied up willy-nilly along the old wharf. "It's his story, or the beginning of it, at least. There's a lot more which I'll show you, if you agree to come aboard."

I kept reminding myself that I didn't need to like Driscoll. He was so pompous.

"I am sure you'd be the first to agree that it deserves to be read and discussed with the patient. We'd like you to take him on. His case. Two months' contract, as I told you. Full time. See if you can crack it."

"But it's fiction, I mean, it's just make-believe. It has to be."

Driscoll turned back from the window. "It's a narrative." He smiled gently. "And you are a narrative therapist."

Yes, I was. And I could do with the money. My overdraft interest was eating its way through my bank account quicker than I could have imagined. I was living in a tiny damp flat over in Ventnor on the South coast. Since I had come back to the Isle of Wight a year earlier, the landlord had increased the rent twice for no reason and without doing any repairs at all. I had no clients. Why was I resisting?

Driscoll's steady gaze and wry smile barely disguised that he knew perfectly well that I had no choice.

"His problems will become very clear after you sign. Frankly, do you really care? Let's be honest, Miss Tench, it will be two months' paid work." He replaced his spectacles and lifted some type-written pages, "Personally, I am more than slightly untroubled by enthusiasm for your discipline, as to its efficacy, just listening to patients' stories. I would have thought that most were very short, aren't they? Just rather badly written short stories of complaint. You know, why I am so fat, why so thin, why I take drugs, how I was abused, why no self-esteem, how I hate my father and so on. Have you actually ever cured anybody at all with your so-called narrative therapy? Does it actually work?" He was looking at my legs. "You are quite young. Australian, isn't it, this narrative therapy stuff, a new-fangled thing?"

I kept a straight face. The question I had to keep firmly suppressed was: *did he know about me*? I was thankful that he didn't seem to, although his gaze rested on my knees just a little too long. I decided he didn't know. I put on my professional voice, trying to subdue my New Zealander accent.

"It helps the patient to identify and step outside their problem. Research has shown that it does work. Definitely so." The *Miss Tench* I had felt to be a put-down, but Driscoll's slur was an insult and was totally unprofessional. A bloody Freudian. After all, we now know that Sigmund Freud, the God of Psychotherapy, thought his wife should be a whore in bed and crushed the life out of her in the process. Prejudiced. Dinosaur, I thought inside my head as I adopted a benign smile and gazed back at him, trying to keep it level, trying to keep the conversation equally balanced with this white-haired, balding, pompous and pudgy old dog in his expensive suit and silly bow tie. His Harley Street background. His plummy Edwardian accent. His nice, safe, part-time, part-retired job on the Isle of Wight. His clean NHS office. His minions. I knew he would wear a banded straw fedora in summertime. Vengeful, I tried to imagine him naked and my smile brightened. I pitied his wife, if he still had one.

"It actually originated in New Zealand."

"Because I think you are in for a rather tough surprise. Adam Doe writes at great length and, if I may venture an opinion, is not a bad writer. He is along from your, er, office there, a bit along the coast from Ventnor. His poor grandmother lives down at Capper's Gorge. She says she really can't cope anymore."

Driscoll looked at his (gold, naturally) watch. "So, Miss Jane Tench, will you please sign up?"

I took the contract papers and he unscrewed the cap and offered me his hefty Montblanc fountain pen, "Please be careful with the nib."

"Just one thing, Mr. Driscoll. If you don't believe in Narrative Therapy, then can I ask why are you hiring me for Adam Doe?" Keep calm, Jane, not petulant.

Driscoll let out a long breath, almost a sigh. He wanted me gone.

"Well. Because we have already tried everything else."

"So I am the last resort?"

Driscoll's cheek muscles lifted beneath the fat. "I'm afraid so. Truly the last resort. Adam Doe believes that he has no escape. We've been told that there's a strong risk he might try to kill himself. We obviously can't be seen to let that happen."

I could see he was thinking about his career and his professional indemnity insurance. About viral complaints on Twitter, Instagram and God knows what else.

"Is there any chance of an advance?" I was winging it.

"Well, it would be unconventional....." He brightened for an instant, "I believe it's an opportunity for you, Miss Tench. After all, you haven't yet published any papers in your field. It may be your chance...." He licked his lips and adopted what he obviously thought was a charming smile. "We may extend the period of your contract if you can make some headway."

Lots of lovely NHS money, paid on time.

"Mister Driscoll. If there was an advance I would feel happier."

"Well then, I'll see what I can do to persuade people." Driscoll handed me the contract and I signed. He took one copy and handed me a thick folder as he moved to open the door. "Let me know how you get on. I'll have my staff post you your official departmental identification and Adam Doe's contact details."

Driscoll turned. "One last thing, Miss Tench. All expense claims must be supported by receipts."

2

I got the bus back to Ventnor, southwards through Rookley, Godshill and Wroxall. The autumn fields were full of tractors, ploughing in post-harvest stubble in dark lines. The sky was overcast. The hills muddy green. Winter was coming and the tourists had gone. The island was closing in on itself and so was I.

Our bus reached the crest of the road at Lowtherville and the Channel spread out deep below us in a flat grey plain, no longer blue. The few slumped local passengers looked at their phones, indifferent to the view. Ventnor huddled in against the sides of St. Boniface Down, a Victorian seaside resort well-attended by tourists in Summer, but now empty, the houses sticking together in dense groups like vertiginous barnacles under the higher woods. The High Street was nearly empty, the usual alcoholics smoking outside the pubs.

The flat on Pier Street was empty too. Empty, damp and dark. Fiona, my illegal flatmate, was out. I decided I could afford to make a cup of coffee, but then to save electricity I forsook the light switch and took the cup and the folder to the table at the window and opened Adam Doe's file in the waning daylight. I re-read the first bit about Captain Pendleton and the strange woman on the Sea Witch. In my few short years of experience in narrative therapy, I hadn't read anything like it. Driscoll, I had to admit, was right. Patients usually kept to their domestic complaints, to be honest. The writing out of their concerns, the theory went, helped them to accept and deal with their emotional problems. This was different. I was sure it was made up. Adam Doe was obviously a druggie with a strong imagination. From my experience, druggies were not reliable at all. Where was it going? It obviously had nothing to do with reality.

But I remembered the fee, poured myself another coffee, switched on the light and turned the page over. It even had a title, the Moondish, handwritten in surprisingly neat copperplate. This spoke of a meticulous, careful person, not at all the careless wastrel that I had imagined in my head. I was ready to be taken for a ride, but, hey, the NHS was paying. Later, I would order a curry. I started reading.

PART TWO

Rosie Cotton

3

<u>Bonchurch, Summer 1849.</u>

The distant hammering had woken her at dawn and had persisted all morning. It came from somewhere by the waterfall round the small headland at the other side of the cove, echoing slightly, muffled in the thin rimey mist which dulled the shore. With the noise, if Rosie Cotton had not been perched on the stool, stooping to catch her reflection close in the tiny window pane, worrying about her summer freckles, she wouldn't have heard the crunch of boots until it was too late.

She fell off the stool when she saw the men coming. She threw down her hair slide and leapt off, crouching down low, breathing fast. Peering just over the sill, she watched the three men coming slowly towards the cottage - dark men, heavy slow boots crunching the round stones like cold grey eggs. She knew from their hats and their pistols - and by their lazy swagger - that they were gobbies, coastguards from the Steephill Station along the coast. They trod the beach three abreast, as if they owned it. Rosie cursed, trying to think. How inevitable that they had come at the worst time possible. If she had just got ready quickly and left, she would have been gone twenty minutes before they arrived.

But she had lingered, smoothing the lace of her smock, her eyes mesmerised by the intricate patterns and the rich creamy colours, holding it up against her, delighting in the shining threads and thickness and folds of the translucent cloth. Smuggled in off the French cutter from Barfleur only the night before, along with thirty pairs of gloves, two boxes of spices, two boxes of tobacco and the twenty four-gallon tubs of pure uncoloured brandy, now hidden in a crack in the cliffs along the shore towards Luccombe Chine, she had agonised over whether to wear it or not. The Frenchman had tossed her the parcel as if it were nothing. "French Blonde!" He had called out, laughing quietly from the skiff at the water's edge, and when she had run down the sand, thinking he had another tobacco box to hand over, he had thrown her the parcel, *"Desormais, je t'apporterais quelque chose comme ça chaque fois que je reviens,"* He chuckled, with a long look at her, "From now on, I'll always bring you something like this, every time I pass by."

Even in the danger now come, Rosie was loathe to let go of the precious material. French Blonde it was called. A pattern of lace which cost a pound weight of silver per pound of lace. Made on the Island by Freeman & Nunn from a pattern which was a priceless and closely-guarded industrial secret, half with machinery at Newport, the capital of the Island, and half with machinery on the mainland in Gloucestershire to stop competitors discovering the intricate pattern.

She peered again through the small window and saw the tallest coastguard with a rough beard and black top-hat, the leader, wave the others forward. She had to act quickly. If they caught sight of her white smock, its delicate embroidery, she knew she would never see her father alive again. In 1849, it was as simple as that. A convicted smuggler would be deported to the colonies or, worse, sentenced to five years in a man o' war of the Royal Navy. In either case Rosie knew that her father would never come home.

Carefully and quickly, Rosie pulled off the smock and frantically looked round for a cleanish sack to carry it in. She couldn't be late for the prize-giving. The new school had just been built, and the village children had been so far accommodated in the coach house of East Dene Manor. This was the last prize day for the old school and Rosie's last day before she had to find work. Soon she would have to go to Newport, the capital market town, and line up with other women and girls on First Bargain Saturday in the High Street at Gape Mouth Corner, hoping that one of the farmers staggering from The Vine would take to her and hire her for the year as a farm servant. At least to be chosen would let her get away from her father at last. The whole village would be at the school for the prize-giving and many of the rich folk over from Newport, and even some visitors from London. A sight of people there would be, truly, she thought with a tightening stomach, feeling her guts go squinny. Her late arrival would be marked down as disrespect and anyway Rosie suspected that she had won a prize. If she had, she wanted to be there to collect it. It could mean that she could ask for a higher wage, on top of the extra value a wealthy farmer would pay her for already being able to write.

Hearing the men outside, Rosie's first thought was that she had no boots and second that a sack was no good. How could she be so stupid? If she was carrying a sack, the men would immediately want to see in it. A booming crash resonated as a thick stick hit the other side of the door. In panic, Rosie thrust her bare feet hard into an old pair of boots which Joe had left behind. Wincing as her toes were squeezed in a gap in the loose sole, she crammed the smock high up underneath her thick skirt and pressed her hand against her hip to keep there. Praying that it wouldn't fall down and show, she walked forward, took the rusting iron key from the lock and held it between her teeth.

With her free hand, Rosie struggled with the latch. She had asked her father time and again to fix it. Bent by the weight of the door and the pressure of endless sea storms, it was difficult for her to push up even with two hands. She could hear the men's impatient voices through the thick planks of the door. The stick crashed down again on the other side. In desperation, she called out as loud as she could, her tongue scraping against the key in her teeth "Just a minute! No need to pelt and swack, you! The hapse is stiff!"

Still gripping the skirt at her hip, she leant hard against the inside of the door and got her thumb under the edge of the rusting bar, pressing it up, her wrist aching with the effort. The sour taste of the rusty key in her mouth made her dribble as she tried to keep her tongue off it, breathing hard as she pushed at the latch. It scraped slightly and then shot up out of its cradle, flinging back the door to reveal the leader with his cane raised up, ready to strike again. He took a step forward, lowered the cane and then motioned the other two back. Rosie recognised one of the men behind, but knew the other two were new men, that they hadn't been bribed and bought off.

"This Cotton's cottage?" The leader growled, raising his scuffed top-hat with cynical contempt. The black hat made him tall in the narrow doorway - tall, strange and forbidding, his head twitching from side to side to see past her head into the cottage, "like a great black flapping bird searching out a worm," Rosie thought.

The familiar Island man stepped forward and spat. "It'n Cotton's neckle alright and a misabul underground duberous sort o' feller he is too. Proberly he's 'n rurfin if you'n axen me." He looked at the leader, "I harken'd vokes say'n they be misabul bad off."

"Rurfin? Meaning what?"

"The ringleader." The third man spoke up, "It'll take you some time to get accustomed to the dialect here, sir." He looked at Rosie, "They've been here so long, it's almost another language." He turned to the Island man, "The master here'll need a linkister to interpret, eh, you?" The man laughed, nodding.

Rosie decided it better to keep speaking in the thick Island dialect, to play the part expected. With luck, she might get rid of them quickly. She curtseyed, her hand gripping the bulge of material at her hip, feeling sick, trying to think of something to say. Her tongue bit against cold iron, sharp rust. Feeling foolish, she took the key out of her mouth, swallowing, wiping away dribble. "Sir, indeed it'n be my father's neckle, but he's presently abroad for a spell, long of the fishing.." she lied, "He'n groyne out since dawn and I proberly shan't see'un till the devil's dancing hours. He does most times." To her annoyance, she felt herself blushing at the lie. "I am about to go out also..."

The leader nodded slowly, seeing the colour in her cheek, not believing her. Under his shaggy eyebrows his little bright eyes were darting around trying to penetrate the gloom of the cottage behind her. "He's gone to Rookley, I suppose."

The other men laughed. "Have you watered it down yet, or is he going to do it there?"

He obviously knew about the latest run of brandy and had been told that the small village of Rookley, in the centre of the Island, was the main point for collection and distribution. Rosie bit back a retort. Nobody would dilute and caramel the brandy before carrying it the ten mile hike over the downs and across the fields into the centre - there was no point in carrying double the weight. But then she realised, of course, the gobbie must have known that. Coastguards were highly trained, like dogs, to the signs and scent of smuggling. Even a short rope brought in with the tubs and carelessly discarded, if found on the floor, was a certain sign of the free trade in brandy tubs and was sure to lead to conviction by the magistrates - the customs men knew that the French twisted the hemp of their tub-ropes the opposite way from ordinary fishermens' ropes.

The two men behind the leader blocked the doorway, openly looking her up and down, grinning. Confident of the upper hand, they expected fun from the confrontation with a defenceless girl. Seeing that they were in no rush, Rosie gripped her stiffening fingers harder and decided to give them no time to enter by force. Flouncing her skirt, she walked straight at the leader, giving him no choice but to step back. Once across the threshhold, Rosie slammed the door shut with her free hand and turned the key in the lock.

"I can't stand yere argufyin with'ee. You'n have to come back tomorrow," She said as pertly as she could, her tongue still thick with rust from the key, trying not to swallow, "I'm late for the parish school, for the prize-giving. Up at East Dene Manor. The Rector will be there, and Captain Swinburne." She saw that her deliberate use of the name had the effect she wanted. She remembered the name of the gentleman who she had been told was going to give out prizes, "and Charles Dickens." The revenue man was duly impressed. By instinct, Rosie knew she had gained the advantage.

"Well then. Tell Cotton we'll be back within the week." The leader snarled. "You tell him that things are soon to change greatly. Things are on the mend! This island has had its own way too long!" He beat his stick against the door in time with each word, "Some Law and Order!" he shouted, "Law and Order throughout the land, even here on this Godforsaken little island, the very edge of the nation! You can tell your stinking father that we're going to clean it up, in the name of her Majesty the Queen."

Laughing, the three turned their backs and strode off on their way to the other end of the cove, towards Horseshoe Bay.

Rosie waited a bit then scrambled across the pebble beach to the beginning of the flint track up the side of the cliff. Sheltered by the gorse at the top, Rosie finally relaxed her grip and splayed her aching fingers, the blood rushing back. Across the cove, the revenue men had paused by the up-turned fishing skiffs below, and were talking to the man who had been banging nails all morning, building a sort of hut directly beneath the waterfall which fell over the cliff-edge. Her impatience made her edgy. She knew she had to stand there behind the bush until they stepped round the headland. Before that, she couldn't risk putting on her smock and move any further.

The gobbies slowly picked their way over the rocks and at last disappeared round the headland. Rosie jerked out the smock and drew it carefully over her head, putting the key in one of the pockets, smoothing it down with her palms. Then she walked quickly up the cliff path and along to the old church behind the trees.

4

Shorter of breath and more flustered, Rosie ran up the steep high-walled lane by the old church graveyard, even though her toes caught in the boot-soles with each step. Not used to wearing anything on her feet at all, she found the boots heavy and clumsy. She hoped that her hardened skin could withstand the rubbing.

As she reached the higher level between the gate of Winterbourne house and the stone bulk of East Dene Manor, the sun suddenly burst through and Rosie paused, catching her breath, enjoying the heat on her back and on the skin of her bare arms. Even the stone masonry lightened, the big entrance of East Dene taking on a mellow softness in the sunshine. Rosie knew the afternoon would be fine. A smart carriage rattled down the lane from Bonchurch village, the two horses turning slowly into the gates under the pointed fan-light between the big round conical turrets. Inside the carriage, she recognised

James Wiskard the master-builder, his bald head framed against the dark red velvet of the interior, calmly looking down at her.

Rosie slid in through the gates after the big wheels of the carriage and stopped, looking around the empty courtyard, where she had played during school lunchtime breaks. She looked at the corner behind the gate where she had waited for her mother, that miserable day long ago when she was told that her mother would never come again. That she was dead and so was the new baby that she and Joe had so much looked forward to. If I win a prize today, she thought, it will be because of mother. Rosie's mother had helped her all the way, from the big first letters and numerals in the battledore, her first primer, to the hesitant wavy scrawl of her first attempt at joined-up writing. She would have been so proud.

Rosie had never been further than the school-room in the coach-house just inside the gates and had no idea what lay beyond. Never having spoken to him, Rosie only knew James Wiskard by sight. But as he had only just arrived, she knew with relief that she couldn't have been late. She heard the rap of the carriage steps unfolding and Wiskard stepped down into the courtyard. At the same time a footman appeared, looking respectfully at Wiskard and then sternly at Rosie. Ignoring the footman, Wiskard bowed low to Rosie with mock solemnity. He raised his torso and reached back inside the carriage, bringing out a gleaming bowler hat. He put it on his head, completing the perfect roundness of him.

Everything about James Wiskard was globular. From the mound of his stomach under the stretched waistcoat to the plump thighs of his sturdy legs. A thin beard joined his chin to his flat ears, like tiny brown feathers stuck to the bottom of a new-laid egg.

He glanced across at the butler standing stiffly to receive him at the entrance. "I'll take the garden route, it'll be quicker," He called back carelessly as he marched over the cobblestones. As he came towards her, Rosie noticed his strange eyes. Round, bulging and unblinking, they had absolutely no expression in them, giving no clue to his thoughts - the pupils fixed tiny and deep in the glass-like balls. More disturbing, as Rosie tried to guess which one he was looking through, was that each eye looked in a different direction - one lazily following the clouds as if in a daydream whilst the other looked directly at her from its red socket, penetrating and perceptive.

"Cotton's girl isn't it?" He started, then fired questions at her, not giving her a chance to answer, "Wonderful day for the prizes, is it not? And a small fete, I believe! Will your father be here today? What's your first name, my pretty little thing?" he paused, wheezing with the speed of his own questions.

Rosie thought for a bit, trying to be polite. She decided it was easier to start with the last question first, and tried to keep in mind the other questions while she answered. "My name's Rosie. Rosie Cotton, sir." She flushed for the second time that day as she curtseyed, noticing with alarm that the eye which had studied her so closely had now relinquished control and was gazing limpidly at the ground between them. The other eye was now studying her, "Yes, sir, my father said he would be coming"

"What a lovely voice you have," He murmured thickly, the eye fixed on her, "Soft and rich...like reeds on the pond up there in the village.... in a gentle summer breeze..." He paused and then lapsed into the Island accent as he quoted from a song, "Your'n hair gleams laike tha' goolden earn, ah' ripplun in t'zun." He said softly.

Rosie was startled at this. Nobody had paid her a compliment before. She had, of course, never considered how her voice sounded to others. She glanced up at him, beginning to see what they meant about James Wiskard. You simply couldn't know what he was thinking. The eyes were no clue - once you thought he was looking at you from one, it went dead and lazy and with a start you found that the other had taken over, craftily waiting on the other side of his big fat nose for you to discover it looking at you, slyly gaining the advantage from your confusion.

He laughed, "Well then, Miss Rosie Cotton, I'll take you in!" Hard fingers gripped her arm, "I'll have to speak to your father later."

Rosie couldn't imagine why Wiskard wanted to talk to her father. Why would a wealthy and well-britched gentleman builder want to speak to her da, who was to her shame known as a drunken sot, a man who would not ask too many questions and kept his mouth shut, a smuggler and a layabout? But then she remembered that Wiskard hadn't always been a gentleman. She had heard along the coastline, catching the women's gossip, that he had grown quickly from being just a foreman at the Pitts quarries up on the downs to becoming very rich, involved in one way or another in nearly all of the construction - the new houses, new villas, new hotels, all built big and solid in thick stone and in elegant style, and the new roads - now rampant all along the sharp rise between the shoreline and the tower of St. Boniface Down, eight hundred feet above. He was even now involved in finishing the construction of the esplanade, the hotels and villas in the new resort at Ventnor, a mile along the coast.

Wiskard almost dragged her along as they walked together through the arch. The gardens were a profusion of colour. Newly-planted only a few years before, Rosie could pick out exotic bushes and flowers and a group of young trees which looked like spread umbrellas, blown out on their spines by the latest gale, which she guessed were palm-trees. East Dene was the grandest of the big new houses. It was built on the site of an old farmhouse and the field which fell below its gardens ended at the very edge of the cliff over the tiny cottage where Rosie lived and was born. The bulk of the down blocked the wind from the north and the sun shone hot and strong from the English Channel.

Unable to get rid of the horrible taste of iron rust left in her mouth, Rosie was grateful not to have to talk to James Wiskard. She was overawed by the crowd gathered on the lawn, content to drink in the rich colours in the women's full silk gowns and parasols and the men's dark formal frock-coats which gleamed like moleskins in the sun. Maids in uniforms - black dresses, white pinafores and little bob-hats - continually emerged from doors behind the open white french-windows to scurry about serving refreshments amongst the soft murmur of polite conversation. It was a scene of complete elegance and harmony, a resplendence of polished grace.

"Intriguing, isn't it my dear?" She heard the wheeze deepen with satisfaction as Wiskard surveyed the huge house and the shining people. "Now it's here, now *they* are here, I find it difficult to remember what it was like before! Just an old farmhouse, just sheep and fields and sea. Nothing else for miles in either direction, all along the coast. Now all gone. Progress!" He smiled down at her, "Only your little cottage remains rotting on the shore, and a few others like it. A reminder of what it was like when," He coughed, "When we were younger. Who would have imagined it could have happened so quickly? Even the Queen herself at Ryde, only a few miles away across the Downs. I've seen her in her carriage, you know!" He was laughing, excited, his wheeze getting faster, "We are going to start building along the coast next, in Sandown Bay. Such Progress! Such Wealth! Where will it end, Eh?"

Yes, thought Rosie, where will it end? It had only started because some fancy London doctor, Queen Victoria's private physician, called Clarke she had heard, had stumbled across the Undercliff by accident on a fossil-hunting expedition and had pronounced that the air was good for chest complaints. Immediately, there had come to a few cottages and farms embedded in pockets and bays along the lonely coastline what her father called "the speculationists"; and the fevered development of a jumbled, sprawling seaside metropolis began. Naked scars were carved willy-nilly in the rise up to the downs above, each scar littered with the debris of the builders around the growing skeletons of the huge houses. The local gossip spoke of unbelievable plans - for cutting a tunnel right through St. Boniface Down for a railway. After the promenade had been built right along the whole length of the sea-front at Ventnor, they were thinking of building a pier. There was even talk of a peeler, a policeman.

Wiskard took her hand and guided her in the direction of the group on the lawn where ladies sat at elegant little tables in the centre, the older ones on upholstered sofas brought out specially from the drawing rooms, their prim figures lost in little bonnets and huge cushions and the flowing lengths of their shining silk dresses. She glanced down at her own scuffed and dirty leather boots beneath her smock, her agitation rising in the face of all that finery. She quickly wiped her mouth with her sleeve, hoping that it had removed any rusty dribble. Rosie was dying for a drink to wash away the twangy taste of rust in her mouth.

Long since they had done any physical work, but still retaining the legacy of it, James Wiskard's pink manicured fingers hid a firm grip as he drew her to the edge of the group on the lawn. He accepted a cup of tea in delicate porcelain. The maid (whom Rosie knew as a recent arrival from one of the inland villages, lucky enough to get a place as a kitchen maid in the new house) looked at Rosie, quickly taking in her loose hair, the rough serge under her lace smock, and her scuffed boots. The maid's chin lifted as she looked down her nose, deciding that it was not proper to serve the young girl with tea - she was definitely not "Respectable" and, even more objectionable, was much younger - and much more pretty. Rosie could see the thoughts on the maid's face. Rosie also saw the maid's bad-tempered alarm when Wiskard loudly made her turn back. "A cup of tea for Miss Cotton would be welcome, if you please!"

Trying to soften the resentment, Rosie smiled and whispered to the maid in their own dialect, "Jest half a sheardful, ef you please. No need to get carky."

But the maid was having none of it, "I b'int in a pucker. I'll get your'n sheard directly. No need to get mouthey, you. You'nt one of this'n Lazy Club!"

Nobody else in the genteel crowd appeared to notice when the maid rudely stomped back, shoving the saucer in her hand, spilling some. Rosie was pleased that nobody was looking at her as she tried to manage her first experience with both a cup and a saucer. She sipped with hesitation, fascinated by the miniature blue figures with scratchy long beards in funny hats on the cup and saucer, crossing little angular bridges under willow trees between intricate little houses. Her father had often pointed out the big tea-clippers with their huge square-rigged sails forging up the Channel, and she had wondered why so much was made of carrying leaves across the world from China, one hundred and twenty days away by sea. She really believed that the leaves must contain something very exotic. She'd heard that kitchen staff kept it under lock and key. She was disappointed at its bitter taste. It wasn't that different from the rust in her mouth. Feeling small and awkward, balancing the half-empty cup on the saucer, Rosie gazed out over the gardens and the field, watching a set of white sails on the long line of the horizon. When she saw one of the elegant ships reaching in with full sail from the Atlantic, its coloured flags signalling its arrival to the Lloyds' Signal Station high up on the down above her, she always thought of her brother, Joe. Every time she saw a ship she wondered if Joe might be on it, hoping that after the few hours that it took by railway from Gravesend or the London docks, Joe would appear at the doorway with his bright smile and broad shoulders in a sailor's jacket with gold buttons. Then they could light a fire under the trees high up on top of the downs, as they had done as children, alone together out of the wind, staying in the firelight until the dawn with her only real friend, listening to his tales of his adventures across the world.

But Joe had never arrived and she had never heard word from him since he had left eighteen months before. Now, as she stood at the edge of the bright crowd waiting for her chance to escape, the sight of a ship only made her feel more lonely than ever. She had no friends because of her father. Even the local children averted their eyes when she passed. Rosie lived in the crumbling hovel perched on the shingle, alone with her father, isolated in the cold wasteland between the land and the sea, trading in smuggled goods between strangers - the strangers on the land and the strangers from the sea. Only Joe had escaped.

PART THREE

Joe

5

<u>The Sea Witch. South Cathay Sea. Summer, 1849.</u>

In the wet hot air a copper sun, a perfect new shining penny, deepened slowly in hue as the twilight rose like dark steam to greet it. The white houses on the shore, the brass rails and binnacles and the deep mahogany of the ship all flamed deep reds and oranges, livid with sunburn. The holystoned and sanded deck, normally a long curve of light cream, shone pink in the declining light.

At last there was a breeze. In the near twilight, a blonde-haired bare-footed young man in baggy, slightly stained, trousers lay stretched-out on his stomach on a hatch cover near the prow. Half-dreaming, Joseph Cotton had watched the girl come down to the small village in the bay and her meeting the Captain and a young Chinese priest. As the tide came in, sluggish little fishing sampans clustered together in the faint swell, getting ready to set out from the stone jetty. He watched them manoeuvre, the rowers standing, pushing at oars lashed to stakes.

Three armed sailors were keeping watch and the Sea Witch was moored for a quick escape in case of trouble, whether trouble came from the sea or from the land. Every week there was drilling of the crew at the guns and in the small arms, with practice with revolvers and rifles, and cutlass exercise carried on under awnings on deck. At suitable intervals, the drill was varied, so that the men were always ready for an emergency and to jump to any necessary weapon. They would be ready to sail, with or without a figurehead. Good luck or bad. It all depended on the Novice Priest on the shore.

Above and in front of him, six sailors balanced their way sure-footed up the huge 60-foot bowsprit, pointing up into the sky above the darkening island. They had already removed the iron bolts from the body of the figurehead and now its scarred form was being lowered into a sampan to carry it over to the island for the promised treatment. The Opium War had been over for several years, but every captain who still ran cargoes of the drug knew well that the dreaded pirate junks could appear at any minute. Only the week before, the oak figurehead had had its head blown off by a cannon shot and the crew now refused to leave without a new one. Joe was only carpenter's mate's mate, not skilled in carving. The Ship's Carpenter Huggins had been rolled into canvas and plunged into the South Cathay Sea quickly after his death to prevent a spread of disease. The Carpenter's mate, Bradshaw, was left and was …..well, unreliable and slow.

It was only after a clicker of a hundred thousand cicadas carried clear across the water, mixed with the occasional harsh staccato clacker of tiles from resumed games of *mah jhong* being played in the open-doored houses on the shore, that Joe realised that there had been complete silence as the meeting had taken place on the quay between the girl and his Captain and the Chinese priest. Everyone must have been watching it quietly. Ten days seemed a very long time to wait when it was so unsafe. True, Captain Doe had sold the cargo off at knock-down prices, but the drug was so expensive that the hold of the Sea Witch still held more than a million Mexican silver dollars to carry all the way back to England. They all prayed for a safe passage.

Joe got up, picked up his shirt and meandered back to the main deck, where the trading had gone on all day. Back between the forward house and the midshiphouse, there stood on one side chests of Patna opium in dark cakes, on the other smaller chests of the highly-prized and more pungent Benares - the finest and most alluring opium from the poppy fields of India. Each had been labelled by the *schroffs*, the bi-lingual Chinese intermediaries, with the name or chop-mark of the purchaser. The drug came in forty balls to a chest, each ball about the size of an apple-dumpling and containing a sphere of crude opium juice, looking like thick treacle, covered in a shell of dried poppy petals.

Between these cases of opium stood a large pair of brass scales, for weighing it out. On a table to one side several smaller scales had been placed to weigh any suspicious dollars.

During the afternoon, sampans had brought case upon case of silver, which were hoisted up and landed on the deck and opened for inspection under the watchful eyes of their owners. The variety and amount of the treasure had, at first, left Joe dumbfounded. Some of the silver was in bars, smooth shining heavy ingots of eight or nine inches in length, but most silver was in *"Maksaigo nganchin"*, as the Chinese schroffs called the mounds of bright Mexican silver dollars. The carpenter had told him that the average price agreed for one chest of the Patna opium was around two thousand dollars, and for the small balls of Benares even more. Some of the Chinese were ragged and poor and had brought baskets containing old silver spoons, broken jugs and tankards and pieces of intricate silver fretwork, which they pushed forward at the schroffs, with loud, spitting proclamations of their value, desperate to buy.

The Chinese haggled long and incessantly and the quarter deck and the main deck had become a noisy floating market place. But once all deals had been struck, the faces of the traders became reflective and austere, as each savoured in his mind the delight of bargains just made and the profits to be looked forward to.

Then came the long and meticulous procedure of checking and counting the treasure. "Watch this here Joseph!" Pausing from his work on the bolts,

Bradshaw the carpenter's mate had pointed to the group of schroffs on the deck. Each of them had the nail of the little finger of the left hand grown to a length of between six and eight inches, like the last talon on a damaged claw. "Kept scrupulous safe and clean," murmured Bradshaw in Joe's ear, "They keep that claw well-hidden in they long sleeves."

Joe watched the serious little men in their dresses and long high-necked jackets with baggy sleeves, their flat-soled soft shoes with up-turned, pointed toes, their shaved heads and pig-tails and their impassive faces. A curious music, a rhythmic dance, began as each man bent to a separate box of silver coin, took one coin out, flicked the long nail against it with a sharp ringing sound and then passed it into the hollow of the hand, up the wrist and into the hanging sleeve of his jacket until fifty dollars had been checked and put aside. Then the dance and the chime would begin all over again, sounding like faint cowbells in the warm air. After being intrigued, Joe had quickly, unbelievably, become bored by the sight of endless silver coins being tapped and counted.

The process was interrupted only once in the afternoon, when a schroff had thrown seven coins in succession on the deck, and turned angrily to confront one of the proud-looking buyers who stood, his arms folded and feet apart, in a red silk robe decorated with a plumed peacock, impassively listening to the jabbered outrage of the schroff.

Bradshaw nudged Joe. "He's been caught! Them coins don't ring true."

The disgraced mandarin began to shout, waving his arms angrily in the air, stabbing his finger at the offending box. But he went quiet enough when he saw two sailors move forward with drawn revolvers. Joe felt Bradshaw's breath in his ear, "You'll never guess who he is! See that small button on the top of his hat? He's one of the Canton Governor's magistrates!" Joe squinted in the light at the gold button on the crown of the mandarin's hat, a sort of skull-cap with a broad upwardly-turned brim, "Just shows you, doesn't it?" Bradshaw chortled, "He's the law and order around these parts!"

The mandarin turned angrily and slid over the rail to his sampan below. Two servants appeared over the rail, nervously kow-towed around them to one and all, grabbed the box and slid over the rail on the heels of their master. At that moment, there was the sound of great laughter from further astern and for a second, Joe thought that the sailors were laughing at the back of the departed mandarin. But then he saw that two sailors had opened up a hatch and were winching something heavy up through the hatchway. After much heaving and turning, a large oblong shape emerged, covered in a large sackcloth, and was swung out to land on the deck with a crash of discordant but unmistakable notes. Everyone burst into sudden, good-humoured laughter, fading as Captain Doe stepped forward. "Men! Lads!" He shouted as the laughter died, "We have done very well here today, and we have sold our full consignment of opium." He drew his hand through his thick white hair and looked around him convivially to loud cheers. "And because we have done so well, there's no need now to proceed up the coast any further. I've arranged for a new figurehead to be carved here by an expert at the temple and once it's ready we'll make way and sail directly up the Pearl River to Canton and Whampoa Island, where we will load with tea. "

The captain moved across and placed a hand affectionately on the side of the large oblong object, "And now we come to what has become known to you all as "Captain Doe's Follies". Yes! I know what you think!" He looked around with good-humour at the men and Chinese. "We will also try our best to sell these little pianos, of which we have no less than twenty-eight in the hold, and which we have shipped here at the insistence of the manufacturer in London who is keen to expand his market in China, in the very earnest belief," Captain Doe pulled a comically wry face, "that China will be a market as big or even bigger than a second India for the British manufacturers - in everything from Lancashire cottons, to Sheffield cutlery" Here again, the Captain made a comical expression as he imitated with his fingers the motion of using chopsticks. Everyone chuckled, sharing the joke," and finally indeed to these pianos!"

With a flourish, he tore off the cloth wrapping to disclose a large crate, from which the side had been removed so that the lid of the piano's keyboard could be lifted and the whole length of the shining ivory keys could be reached. "Now," The Captain looked across at the Chinese traders, "If you gentlemen would care to listen, I have asked the Doctor to demonstrate these wonderful instruments. And, should you wish to purchase one, then I will be very happy to discuss a price with you."

The ship's doctor came forward with a stool, sat his thin body down at the crate, crouched over the keyboard and passed his fingers slowly over the length of the keys. Satisfied that it was in tune, he began to play. As everyone fell silent, his reedy voice lifted in a hymn, tinged with his soft Dublin accent.

"Eternal Light! Eternal Light,
How pure the soul must be" Sang the doctor.

After the opening bars, the Englishmen began to feel the sadness of the wistful, lilting melody. Some shamefaced at the emotion, carefully avoiding each other's glances, they all shared the ache planted by the simple tune, reminding them all of home, so very far away. One by one, they joined in humming the tune, acknowledging their sadness, thinking of their families, trying to conjure the faces of those they had left behind. The Chinese had fallen silent and stood together, naturally had formed a line in polite puzzlement, eyes downcast until the strange ceremony was over.

"The spirits that surround thy throne, May bear the burning bliss; But that is surely theirs alone, Since they have never, never known,
A fallen world like this."

Suddenly acutely homesick, Joseph was thinking of his sister, Rosie, trying to imagine her, trying to see her face, what she was doing, seeing her run along the pebbly shore outside their cottage under the Bonchurch cliffs, back home in the Isle of Wight. He held her in his mind for as long as he could, before the image started to dissolve, her face as he had last seen it, frightened, tearful and anxious in the dawn light, waving goodbye as he finally shouldered his sack, turned his back and set off along the track towards the ferry at Ryde. She said she understood that he had to leave, that he had no choice. But still he felt guilt about leaving her there with their father. Ever since the *Sea Witch* had left the London Docks, he had saved all the money he could so that when he got home he and Rosie would be able to move away, maybe even off the Island altogether.

"There is a way for man to rise
To that sublime abode:
An offering and a sacrifice,
A Holy Spirit's energies,
An advocate with God. .... "

There was silence when the hymn had finished. The doctor let the resounding final chord languish and die in the heat. They all stood, held by the spell. Then, to ease the mood, following his own private reverie, the Doctor began the wistful lament of a nocturne by Chopin, the shining notes falling and melting like ice flakes on a shore which had never seen snow.

PART FOUR

6

Shame

It was the stillness which Grin Ling Chen remembered afterwards. The South Cathay Sea glittered silver and flat. The midday sun had driven the sea air into dense blue shadows under the island trees and the cicadas had stopped their clatter in the bushes above the bay. Chen stood breathless from his run down from the hill, his nose running, scratching the spread of itchy skin under his linen and his special silk coat which the servant Yip had made him put on to impress the foreign Captain.

The tide ebbed East. The still air soaked the silence, thick with the smell of fish pinned up to dry on bamboo poles slung along the small quay.

Chen squinted in the light and shaded his eyes. The Captain was being rowed ashore in a dinghy. His western ship slept at anchor in the bay, tall masts and spars like hangman's gibbets, sails hung in the wet air like filthy rags. The gash in the figurehead at her prow, the wooden head severed and hanging by a thin strand of split oak. The ship had limped in to the bay without warning and servant Yip, always quick to spot an opportunity for making money with the minimum of personal effort on his part, had burst into Chen's workshop and dragged him away from the screen which the Priest had ordered him to finish carving before his return by sampan from Canton.

"Superstitious, these foreigners." Yip chuckled weasily as they went down the track from the Temple to the quay. "They have bad luck. But their bad luck will be our good fortune!"

Your good fortune, thought Chen. But then, with just a little bit of luck, he might be able to get enough from the foreigners to pay the Temple servant to keep his mouth shut. If Chen could be clever, his guilt could disappear like morning mist under a rising sun. Guilt was personal, shame was public. He would replace the gold and vermilion which he had sold to pay for the black foreign mudpaste. When the Priest returned from Canton, nobody would know. If he was clever.

His chisels were sharp and the files from the cloth bag laid out carefully in order of size on the stone bench beneath the window of the Temple workshop. But he had to think carefully - there was only camphor wood, no oak, no cinnabar, no mercury or sulphur, so after the carving was finished the painting would have to wait. There was no gold or red vermilion left because he had sold them in return for a ball of opium. Would the foreigners have any paint themselves? What colours would they demand?

The rowers held their oars aloft, the ship's dinghy scraped the dark muddy shingle and the Captain was helped ashore, just as Chen caught another movement. The figure of a young English woman was being helped over the side of the boat, stumbling a little, one hand raised to the dark veil which covered her face, a thin line of sweat in the cloth at the pit of her arm, the other hand clutching a thin book and, with the spare fingers, the hem of her long black dress to keep it from the muddy shingle. She gained the edge of the quay and walked up the slope, then stood watching as the Captain and his mate walked up to Chen and Yip, the other sailors spreading out in a protective circle, hands on pistols.

Keeping a respectful distance from the Captain and his group, Chen watched the English sailors under lowered eye-lids, some sitting on the quay parapet, some standing close to their captain.

"Well enough then. Our carpenter was not practised in the art and he is mmmh....sadly now dead from dysentery." Captain Doe shrugged his heavy shoulders, "We have his mate but his skill at carving is insufficient." He nodded his head at the ship. "Our ship must have its figurehead remade before it can sail. More bad luck otherwise, as my crew insist." The Captain smiled. "It is a common fancy that the figurehead embodies the spirit of the ship and it must be restored before we make way."

Yip pointed at Novice Chen, "We have this young man to carry out the task. Very skilled. He called Chen Grin Ling, so he good. Grin Ling Chen. Like Grin Ling Gibbons."

"For how long must I be detained with him?" The girl pronounced the words slowly, as though she had had to arrange every word in her throat before she said it. Novice Chen wanted to see her face. It would be difficult enough carving a Western face. A round head, round eyes, large nose. Why the veil?

The Captain turned to Chen, "*Do Jiu mah?*"

Chen could barely understand the Captain's Chinese through his blackened teeth and thick yellow beard – a mixture of mandarin and Cantonese, it sounded cobbled and his accent was bad. His breath smelt of ale and tobacco, even at two yards. For Chen, stepping back, the Captain's stink was worse than the smell of the dead fish in the heat. He paused, smiled to show he meant no offence, bowed slightly, then answered in English, "I must see kind lady's face before I can judge how long job will last."

"Miss? He will need to see your face." The Captain realised his bluntness and made an effort at diplomacy, "Modesty must succumb to necessity, if you please."

The girl stiffened and splayed her fingers on the hips of her dress. Her book dropped in the dust and its covers flew open, pages opened in the light, like a strange 3-petalled flower. One page black, the next white and the last red. Chen could see there was no writing. It was a simple three-coloured thing.

Chen stepped forward to retrieve it but the girl squatted, grasped the book and clasped it to her thin chest. Standing, she let her shoulders go slack as she bent her head and turned it away, "Suppose, then so be it, as you wish." Her voice had deepened and the eight oily words clumped together in her throat. "Indeed." She paused, clutching her book. Then, as if reciting an instruction learnt by heart, "It is because I am but the solitary English woman here and must serve as a form for your work."

She slowly brought her fingers up to the veil, "But you will have to be skilled." She pulled it up and raised her head, her eyes defiant. "You will have to be very skilled."

The Captain, a big man muted, held her gaze and tried not to turn his head to look at Chen.

"So. Will I suffice?" She stood straight and her tone dared them. She waited for their verdict calmly, almost with sympathy, expecting their dismay, "I keep the veil to spare our weaker brethren."

The blistering rash covered half of the right side of her face. From her eyelid down to just above her mouth, the blemish flared dark rust, mottled and raw against the pallor of her face. Whatever, whoever, had done it, she must have been in agony for days. To Chen it looked like an acid burn. Her hair, straying from under the veil, was the colour of light pine wood. Her eyes had a slightly startled look, wide and round, a dark amber brown, shining as the skin of a chestnut freshly prised from its shell, the underlid of the right eye slightly sagged above the top of the flaw.

She cannot be more than seventeen years old, Chen thought, but the scar disfigurement, and her resignation, made her seem older.

Chen took a small pace forward, hiding his distaste, feigning interest in noting proportions. He would have to thicken the line of the neck to make a strong and seamless join with the figurehead's wooden body, give her fine cheekbones, a full mouth, a firm jut of her chin. She could then sit well at the front of the ship. It would be simple to carve her face without the rash. By taking care and concentrating on the facial crevices, Chen reflected, he was sure he could capture her round eyes and her strong nose and, well, he could falsify the rest.

Satisfied, Chen let his eyes drop, pulling his long oiled pigtail from behind his shaven head so that it fell across his shoulder. His training told him not to offer an opinion, to remain aloof, keep his distance, keep objective, but the girl's spirit had moved him in a way which he didn't welcome. He lifted his gaze to confront hers.

"You will suffice much. Very. Thank you."

She looked surprised. Chen noticed what he thought was disappointment as she looked down at her feet. Would she be difficult? He would have to allow for that possibility. These foreigners were arrogant, everyone knew. Their fast ships and powerful cannons and their wordless books and their bibles. And their Indian opium.

Yip turned to the Captain. "Ten days."

The Captain waved an arm over the island, its small hills, the shallow bays, the scrub bushes. "We're not protected here. Three days, no more."

"Four days with painting. Seven hundred Mexican silver dollars for the Temple."

The Captain swallowed noisily, pulled at his beard, his little wrinkled eyes withdrawn as he considered bargaining. Chen cut into the Captain's thought, "And a chest of opium."

"But we have today sold the last of our opium!"

"Then sir, respectfully, you will have to make a re-purchase for me." Did he push too far? Yip was looking at him angrily. But Chen could not afford the shore price and he desperately needed a good supply. The price of opium in Canton was so far out of his reach. He waited, sniffed and scratched himself again. The Captain took a step closer to Chen. "You are sure you can finish the job?"

Chen started to sweat, anxiety cramping his gut.

He knew the paint would be a problem. He had some lacquer but didn't have the lead white or vermilion. He would have to find something else. The ship would be long gone before the foreign devils noticed anything amiss. "You have an oak block?"

"We have it." The Captain raised his hand to shade his eyes, looking deep into Chen's. He had noticed the tiny black pupils, pin-pricks. "So. If I buy you some opium to get you started?"

The Captain gave a quarter-smile, his voice soft with sympathy, but his intention hard. "And you accept one chest and three hundred Mexican silver dollars for the Temple in full payment?"

Chen couldn't stop the wide yawn coming but quickly raised his hand to cover it. He knew when he was beaten. But once he had the opium in his pipe, the cramps would go, he would be able to sleep, the sweating and the yawning and vomiting and diarrhoea would stop and he would be able to start the job. And, with luck, it could be much quicker. "One hundred extra for early completion – for every day below four days."

He could feel the girl's eyes on him. Her cool regard. Was it contempt? Why did he care what she felt? He blundered, "And one hundred for the girl." What was he doing? Yip was not looking at him, but Chen could feel his anger at losing control of the negotiation.

"No." She whispered. "For our Mission. It must be."

Chen looked at the Captain.

"Agreed." The Captain grunted the word like a pig.

"I will take measurements today and we will start tomorrow morning at my workshop in the Temple." Chen turned, "If that is convenient for you, Miss?"

She quickly pulled the veil down over her face. "Alice…Alice Capper." Her words were muffled by the veil. Softer. Almost ghostly.

Chen turned to the Captain. "And the name of the ship?"

"Her name is *Sea Witch*."

As Alice Capper turned her back and walked away, Chen noticed that the silence had gone. He could hear the cicadas again. The tide lapped the shore, a soft hiss in the distance, an echo of the busy insects, like a memory of reluctant praise.

7

The Holy Land

Alice Capper had declined his offer of pork and rice with a quick shake of her head. Chen watched her covertly as she sat silently in the corner, her veil down. She didn't seem to feel the morning cold in the workshop. She held her coloured book tightly in her lap, her wordless book with its three pages – the black page, the red page and the white page, pausing at each and then slowly turning from one to the other, as if in a reverie. She seemed to be rebuffing him, almost as if she knew about the dream he had had after sucking in the opium smoke through his pipe the evening before in his bed, its warmth and comfort luring him into a confident assurance of how to convert her face into the beauty and terror of a Sea Witch. Under the caress of his fingers, her face had come alive, shedding her coldness and its scars, her eyes bright, her skin warm, her fair hair shining as it fell across her naked shoulders.

Novice Chen sucked in the chill of the morning, deep and slow to ease his lungs, warming his delicate fingers on the rim of his tea-bowl to stop them shaking, looking out through the Temple columns down the wide steps to the sea beyond. The black English glue medicine had worked well. The light was brighter, the colours more crisp. He felt a readiness in the air. But could he transform her scarred face into the face of the Sea Witch? He smelt the sharp camphor oil on his fingers, unwrapping his small chisels and files from the cloth bag and laying them out carefully in order of size and shape on the stone bench beneath the window of the workshop. The English glue smoke would keep him calm and the camphor allowed him to stay awake and breathe normally. He tried to recall his dream.

The oak block stood before him clamped in position against the stone bench, twice his height, already sawn into the size required for the figurehead. He waited until a tremor passed and he was ready to climb the bamboo scaffold and concentrate on first the outline passes and then later the fine detail as he held last night's dream in his head, its images forming cuts in his mind as he looked at Alice and motioned for her to raise the veil and remove it completely from her head.

"Missee Alice. Please lift veil."

Alice slowly did so and looked up. Her clear gaze. Her resignation. He was pleased to see that she had pinned her hair up, showing the shape of her head in a way that was easy to carve. Chen was already seeing her inside the block of wood, as if her image from his dream waited meekly in the wood for him to cut her free and tell her story.

Humbled, Chen picked up a broad-blade chisel and a heavy hammer. "For the Captain I make your image good. Your spirit will rule the sea. A goddess!"

"I am flesh and that is oak. And that is all."

"But I will take your spirit. Restore your spirit. The Captain has need of it. He pay good Mexican silver."

"Idolatry is a sin." She twisted the thin book in her hands, her voice deadpan. "You shall not carve idols for yourselves in the shape of anything in the sky above or on the earth below or in the waters beneath the earth; you shall not bow down before them or worship them."

Chen suddenly dreaded the next few days. Would she really preach at him like this? His last night's dream of capturing her spirit left him shadowed. The lightness had gone. It was like speaking to an alien creature, her belief closed round her mind like an iron mask, hard and unmoving. It would show in the carving. Irritated, he placed the chisel on the oak and hit home with the hammer with regular careful blows.

But then, he remembered, she had suffered, had brought him luck and the least he could show was a little kindness. "Would you like some tea?"

A tiny smile. A glimmer of warmth. "I admit I have a strong thirst."

Chen called out for Yip to prepare tea, hoping he would boil fresh water and not use the rancid stewed tea from this morning. He replaced the chisel on the oak and hit again with sharp rapid movements. Maybe he could find some warmth in her, some vigour. Some hope.

"You have come a long way. And now you can go home."

Her clear gaze darkened, hardened. "I have no home."

"England?"

"England is no home to me."

"But Miss Alice. Where were you born?"

She gave a small shudder. "I was born in a London slum. An evil, filthy, stinking place called the Holy Land."

Chen tapped away, patient, letting the pause lengthen.

Alice leaned forward. It was the first time that she had volunteered any information about herself.

"There was an act of kindness. I was saved by an act of kindness. A gentleman. A truly gentle man." She paused, thinking back, murmuring to herself, "An act of kindness is an antidote to evil in this world."

Grin Ling Chen stopped chiselling, stood back, admiring his work, only half listening to her, "Who was he, the gentle man?"

"He was a writer of books, a writer of texts," Alice replied.

Her face softened beneath the scars.

"His name was Charles Dickens."

PART FIVE

8

I had completely forgotten to order my curry. It was way past midnight. Fiona had not appeared and I was glad. But I was hungry. I could hear loud voices outside the pubs in Pier Street. I went to the fridge and found half a pork pie and a carton of milk. I could have done with a cigarette.

I had never read anything like it. I wanted to get to the end. What had Alice Capper to do with Rosie Cotton? It was as if Adam Doe knew Rosie's story very well, almost as if he had met her. What was going to happen? Fuck! What the hell was I going to do with Adam Doe? Munching the pie with one hand and drinking the milk with the other, I went back to the story.

9

A huge meal was laid out on trestle tables and on one of the skylights and many bottles of champagne, sauterne, porter and good London Bass ale were served. Joe was given a plate and a glass. The Chinese seemed to appreciate the food and wine, although they had to be coached carefully with knives, forks and spoons and still bent at the waist jerkily with each mouthful, not trusting the food to stay on the fork.

The sun had gone down and in the afterglow candles had been lit all along the rails around the mid-deck. The distant cicadas and murmured conversation of the sailors and traders emphasised the absolute stillness in the air as a transplendent full moon began its rise. The broad fan of its light spread and rippled over the water, reaching out to the ship. Out of the corner of his eye, Joseph caught a flash of phosphorescence shimmer and die towards the jetty. He caught it again and saw a small sampan, slowly rowed as it turned furtively towards the *Sea Witch,* the light and shimmer glancing off the oarblades as they dipped and rose, dipped and shone. In the boat two figures stood, silent and still, either side of a long dark box housed lengthways. The small boat glided stealthily across the water's space towards him.

Joseph turned back to face the deck. His mouth full of roasted chicken and potatoes and his reticence loosened by two glasses of sauterne, Joe finally asked the carpenter a question which had grown in his mind as he watched the unimaginable wealth nailed up in the cases and sealed by the captain, whilst a schroff busily wrote the mounting tally in a leather book.

"Why do they pay so much for it?" He asked, "What does the opium do for them?"

The carpenter looked at him for a long time, then balanced his own plate and glass on the rail, and looked over the dark water towards the small village. He picked at the hard skin on one palm of his hands, and then fumbled for his pipe and tobacco.

"It kills them." He said, flatly, and cleared his throat with a short cough and spat over the rail. "And you should hear the missionaries rant! From Amoy to Foochow and up to Shanghai! But the Chinese mandarins are so corrupt and the profits are so huge for them and for the owners of these ships, and the pay so good for such as the likes of me, that I do not think the trade will ever finish. Did no-one tell you when you signed up why the pay was so good?" He asked, "Didn't you think about it?" His voice had become taciturn, wishing to share a little of his guilt.

"No." Joe muttered. He hadn't thought about it. Looking away, he noticed the sampan with the two figures and the box had disappeared from view in the shadows beneath the bowsprit.

Pipe in mouth, the carpenter pulled back the corners of his eyes **and** mimicked the Chinese pidgin English, "Muchee likee dollar, muchee likee opium, mandarin muchee likee opium sellee, makee dollar. Here, doctor!" He yelled across the deck, "Come and tell Joseph Cotton here. Come over and tell him about what we're selling here!"

The doctor came away from a group of officers and Chinese and reluctantly joined them by the rail. "What is it?" he asked shortly.

The carpenter's manner softened in the presence of the doctor's authority. "Joe here wanted to know about the opium," He mumbled, "That is, now we've sold it all."

"Well, Mr. Cotton," The doctor said, addressing Joe, his Irish tone not unkindly, "I suppose now is as good a time as any to learn what you're involved in."

The doctor paused and leant his back against the rail. He began speaking mechanically, as if delivering a lecture to the both of them about something of academic interest. "The white poppy is grown in India, as you know. During ten days of its annual life-cycle, the seed-box of the white poppy exudes a milky juice of a quite extraordinary chemical complexity, which we still do not fully understand." A few other sailors sauntered over and stood in a circle, holding tankards.

"Tell 'em all straight, doctor." Said the carpenter, under his breath.

The doctor ignored him and continued in the same disinterested tone. "From this milky juice is derived a granular powder, bitter to the taste. From it, we derive the tincture known as laudanum, which is used in solution as a painkiller, very effective for tooth-ache and the like. In fact, it is widely used at home as an effective remedy in certain brands of medicine, such as Godfrey's Cordial and Mother Bailey's Quieting Syrop for Noisy Babies and Children." He gazed at the group in an avuncular way, thinking that he had finished.

At this, Joe saw the carpenter's face grow red and blotchy, suffused by alcohol and anger. "Now tell him the truth doctor, don't stop there, doctor. Tell us about the smoking, tell about the trade."

The ship's doctor looked uncomfortable. "Well," He began, feeling his way, trying to ignore the emotion introduced by the carpenter, clutching for the professionally disinterested voice, "Well, the taste of the powder is repugnant and its absorption into the body is slow. However, if it is smoked, these disadvantages are overcome." He shifted his weight from one foot to another and leant back against the rail again. "The smoker dips a needle into the prepared extract, dries it over a flame and puts a bead of the flame-dried opium into a tiny pipe-bowl of tobacco. The smoke reaches the blood-stream through the lungs, giving an immediate effect...."

"What is the effect, doctor?" Asked Joe.

The doctor began to look trapped. He looked about him for a chance to escape from the group.

"Tell him what the effect is." Growled the carpenter and a few others murmured their agreement, pressing forward.

"I don't know why you men are suddenly so concerned! Suddenly so holy! You've known about it long enough, and have been well enough paid!"

The carpenter leant forward. "It must have been the hymn that you sang, good doctor." He jeered. Some of the others laughed, others looked uncomfortably at their canvas boots. One man pulled at his belt, eyes downward.

The carpenter drank again, and swallowed. "For myself, if I could any other way have had the exciting and adventurous life of this trade, I would have preferred it of course, but I have a wife and three daughters in London to feed and clothe, and "the navy services" in England are only for the rich and the aristocratically born, as you know well."

"In any event," said another, "We wouldn't be drinking good claret and sweet sauterne in the Royal Navy, or be so well looked after....."

They all murmured in consent. Joseph mumbled in agreement, although inside him the justification which the carpenter offered sat uncomfortably in his gut.

"Thank you for your honesty." said the doctor. "Now we all know what we're talking about, I will be pleased to describe it to young Joseph here. What we are talking about, Joseph, what we have done here today, is this. We have helped in the ruin of, say..." His eyes ran over the chests stacked up in the shadows on the other side of the decks, "several hundred thousand Chinese lives, at least, not counting the families of the addicts. Of course, if you count those as well, you could say we are in the business of ruination of up to one million lives with just that cargo which you see there in front of you."

All listening remained silent.

"The first few grains give a wonderful sense of euphoria. But then listlessness sets in. Then, in order to face life again, you would have to make a crucial decision. To leave it alone or to go on repeating and increasing the dose. The general view is that it only takes one pipe a day for only seven or ten days to leave one in the complete grip of addiction. Then the rate climbs to three pipes a day. From then on, one is entering into the very gates of hell..."

"Just one day without it will bring acute symptoms of withdrawal from the narcotic." He held up his fingers, counting them off one by one, "Giddiness, watery eyes, torpor, a permanent chill felt over the whole body, aching in all your limbs to the very bone, appalling diarrhoea and, of course, agonising misery... So the only choice is to continue, until eventually," The doctor shut his fist, saying simply, "Until eventually you die."

"But why?"

"Why? Joseph. A very good question. Anyone here like to answer that question?" The doctor looked around him. There were no takers. He held the floor.

"It is, as always, because of money." He sighed, "Money, trade and politics. That ungodly trio. And their master, the Balance of Trade."

"What do we bring back home from here, Joseph, apart from the pianos which we will not be able to sell?"

Joe recalled the captain's words, "Tea." He said.

"Well then, there you have it in a nutshell. *Tea.* The very tea which the British demand by the millions of pounds in weight every year and drink by the millions of gallons every year. The most valuable herb in the world. The British were buying so much tea and silk from China that they were carting millions and millions and millions of silver dollars by the ship-load to that small port up there," He pointed North into the night sky, "in Canton at the end of the Pearl River."

"The problem was, put simply, that the British were running out of silver. But they still wanted their tea and the British government still wanted the tax on its import! So, Joseph," The doctor put his arm round Joseph's shoulder, "They had to find something that the Chinese wanted to buy!"

"But could they find it? No! *Because the Chinese had everything they wanted.* They didn't want to buy anything from the British. Not cotton, not clothing, not cutlery, not pianos! Nothing! Until," The doctor wagged his finger, looking around his audience, and then tapped his long thin nose, "Until they thought of opium. In opium, they found something that the Chinese would crave as much as the British craved their tea, but because it is an addictive drug, the more they get the more they want. And since then, what happens is that the British, and the Americans it may be said, buy the opium in India cheap, ship it here, sell it off expensive, use some of the money to buy shiploads of tea cheap, ship the tea back to East India Docks in London and sell expensive. That way, the Chinese lose silver instead of the British, the shippers make untold profits, the British government gets it tax and everyone is happy. Except, of course, the millions of Chinese who are hopeless addicts. That clear enough for you, Joseph?"

"Yes. Yes it is. Thank you." His politeness belied the turmoil in his mind. All he had thought about was the excitement of sailing in the wonderful ship, of the exotic destinations, of the high pay. How had he forgotten so easily that there would be a price? Should he have asked before? What difference would it have made? He caught himself at the thought - that was what he found so horrifying in the others - that mental shrug of the shoulders by the traders in death.

Funnily, Joseph sensed that everyone who had listened seemed to relax, as if they had got something off their chests by listening. A silly thought entered his mind. "Is it really the same thing as they put in Mother Bailey's Quieting Syrop For Noisy Babies And Children?"

"Yes, Joseph, indeed it is." The doctor shrugged. "But nobody has seen fit to regulate the use of laudanum as a medicine at home. And life is cheap at home, as you know, cheaper almost than it is here."

Confused, Joe took his plate and glass back to the tables. But maybe it was the wine that was making him confused. Then again, maybe more wine would help. As Joseph stood respectfully behind the captain, waiting to proffer his glass to the galley-steward for a refill of the sweet Sauterne, the first mate came quickly up the stairwell and knocked Joe's elbow as he rushed past him. "Sir, the barometer is acting strange and very curious!"

10

The Blood of the Son

The three days had passed. The carving was nearly finished and Chen was proud of his work. The figurehead stood nearly seven feet tall in the centre of the chamber and he had brought her to life. He had made Alice beautiful. Her face unblemished beneath an ornamental tiara of thorns. Truly a goddess of the sea, her long robes falling across her breasts, draping backwards as if rustling in the breezes. It was his finest work. Only one more session to go to smooth the last tiny rough edges and begin the painting. But no red vermilion to put on under the final coats of lacquer. And Alice and the Captain were expected soon.

He had purchased some gold paint but what about the vermilion? Chen felt his knees lose all strength and he sat down hard on the Priest's bench in the centre of the inner room. He must finish or he would expect no more money, if he had read the Captain correctly. Winded, he looked up just as the idiotic temple servant Yin entered to usher a native woman in. The irritation at being kept back from his work was sharpened by self-doubt. How could he have forgotten that she was coming? As the servant bowed low to him, Chen knew by the fraction too long that he stayed bowed that the servant was laughing at his lack of composure. Chen really wondered how the Priest could have expected Chen, only a Novice, to cope in his absence with this insubordinate servant, who had already shamed Chen by spreading news of his mistakes amongst his drinking companions in the village and was now after any chance to look for a fresh situation for Chen to demonstrate his lack of authority and his incompetence, no doubt so that a full list could be got together before the Priest returned. Chen caught the glint of malice in the servant's eyes as he straightened up and held the door back with his hand. "Let's see what you can do with this one!" The servant's eyes sneered.

But as the woman inched her way through the small doorway, Chen forgot the servant. The woman carried her desolation around her like a black cloak.

She was tall for a Chinese woman, tall and frail, her unbound hair fell in a shining black curtain over her shoulders and down her straight back, shimmering with a gloss caused, he guessed, from not having been able to wash it during her journey. To leave her hair down like this was so unusual that Chen recognised it as a mark of defiance, the mark of the dispossessed, a rebel. She had beautiful eyes, of an unusual deep brown, curved like a cat's and set perfectly above the fragile fullness of exquisite cheekbones. Her beauty was sharpened by her dark clothes, faded, stained and dirty. Remembering the gestures used by the Priest, Chen grandly motioned her to sit. She looked surprised at his youth. Her eyes were full of disbelief that one so young could help her. Chen could see that she was struggling with equal parts of supplication, the remains of hope, and resignation - waiting for him to confirm her fears and for the edges of her hope to shrink suddenly, and evaporate like damp on a wet stone held in the sun. He had seen that expression so many times, in so many eyes during his long training, in many hundreds of faces of desperate people who had come to his master for help. Since the end of the first Opium War with the foreign barbarians, hearing of his master's growing reputation as a doctor and priest, of his wisdom and deep sympathy, they had come from all over South China, some from as far north as Shanghai and Nanking, running from the war, starvation, disease, corruption, persecution and the slow collapse of the Empire and all the old traditions, as the government in Peking and its network of mandarins and petty officials sank into visible confusion and helplessness in the face of the guns and drugs brought by the great ships of the westerners.

But, as the servant had already whispered to him in a rare moment of support, there was something different, dangerous, about this woman. She lowered herself painfully with the aid of a stick, gasping with pain, stretching her feet outwards straight towards him for comfort. Her feet were not bound. Despite her pain, she had walked erect as she entered, not hobbling and bent as most Chinese women did who had had their feet bound and disfigured since birth.

There was something that he sensed strongly. Her eyes gleamed with it in the light of the oil lamp. Hatred. Hard, naked and unashamed. Hatred and the need for revenge. The despicable servant had muttered her story to him, whispered close in his ear with his reeking breath, as the woman waited in the outer rooms. But to the servant she had only hinted why she had really come.

She was of the Hakka tribe, from the Kwangsi district, a wild province of mountain and jungle lying inland on the extreme south-western edge of China, where women worked alongside their men as equals. Or would have, if there had been anything to work with, Chen thought with irony. For Kwangsi, everyone knew, had suffered three successive years of drought and famine. Always known for their hatred of the Manchu Emperor and the Tartar foot soldiers with which they still tried to keep the Empire under control, the Kwangsi Hakka had refused to shave their heads and grow pigtails - a visible expression of their contempt for the Manchu.

The servant entered with bowls of tea and glanced nervously at Chen as he slid back across the threshold and closed the door silently behind him. Chen sat still, trying to recall his master's usual questions. The cicadas rattled in the bushes outside the temple and all the way up the hill behind it as the sun strengthened. In front, through the small door and the outer chamber, they could hear the surf caress the shore in the thickening heat. The moist air was still, tense. Chen, too, felt unusually tense, sweating slightly under the cool silk of his dark robes.

"*Ngo yiu hwa Lao-she.*" She said, speaking to him in the Guangzhou dialect, "I wanted to speak to the High Priest." She took out a small porcelain jar and laid it on the stone bench beside her. Unglazed, white with no pattern or markings.

Chen watched the aura of energy surrounding her body, bright as crystal in the gloom of the chamber. "My Master is not here. He may not return for many days."

"Then I must make do with you. Therefore knowledge of the required depth I hope you have." She had kept her voice soft, but the challenge was there. From any normal person, what she had said would have been extremely rude, to any of the priesthood brethren, let alone a novice now on the point of full brotherhood after being trained from the age of six. Chen knew this, but mentally consigned his pride to a sealed-off corner in his mind. After all, she was Hakka. In accordance with lessons learnt over eleven years of training with his master, Chen kept his mind and all his senses open and heard in her voice other things with the challenge. She was desperate. She had no time and she would ask for his help, despite his youth. Uncompromising, he thought as he glanced at her quickly from under his eyelids, so uncompromising. She had come with a single purpose and was determined to carry it out. Her purpose was all that she had left. She had been a member of the Taiping, but they had failed her and cast her out. She was a renegade Taiping. Had lost her home, family, living, religion, belief. She stood aloof, an outcast at the very edge of civilisation, beyond help, with absolutely nothing left that could be taken away from her. He felt threatened, uneasy, the stone chamber felt unusually humid and close, the heat making him conscious of his sweat. He asked her to repeat her story, listening carefully, trying his best to gauge the depth of her emotion as she spoke, as he had watched his master do a hundred times. In a low voice she told the story again. Of her destitution in the famine, how her husband and two sons had gone to Thistle Mountain and joined the Taiping rebels of Hung Hsiu-ch'uan - the King of the Christian God Worshippers - and his thousands of followers who had forsaken the Emperor, Buddha and Confucius, who had promised salvation in the wake of famine, pestilence and oppression under a divine commission to exterminate the Manchus.

At first on their return, her menfolk had complied with the Taiping rules of self-denial. But then, first her husband and then her eldest son, their resolve had slipped and they had reached for the opium pipe. The drug had used up all the farm money, the creeping listlessness which prevented her men from harvesting, the rice rotting in the mildewed swamp, how they had finally sunk in agony of their own as they could no longer pay for the drug. How they had returned to the rebel's camp for help, had been spurned and disowned because of illness, addiction and disease.

"Desperate," she said, "I travelled back to the farm with the two addicts, and my youngest son, the strongest of us all, my only remaining hope, who kept us all alive by begging for food for us on the road. But when we reached Guangdong, we suffered the final sin and the final ruin. My younger son was arrested by the Manchu Tartars and imprisoned as a rebel and a traitor. We managed to follow them as he and all the other prisoners of good health were taken to the markets." She choked, the reminder forcing a pause. She held her breath, keeping the sobbing back, eyes looking at the floor. After a long time of silence she spoke more slowly and clearly, without feeling, unmoved, as if relating the story of someone else, "The last time I saw my healthy son, he was naked, crammed with others behind the bars of a bamboo barracoon, being hoisted onto an American ship with the flower flag. He was staring down at us. All of them had been stripped naked. They were all painted on their chests and backs with the same big character in red paint," She raised her arm and described in the air the shape of a capital C, "Coolie. Californee-ah. *Meigwok.* America." She muttered. "As the barracoon was raised high in the air by the grinning, stinking barbarians, as he looked down at us, his wretched family, and as I looked up at him, we knew we were finished. We would never see each other again." Her voice faltered. Another long pause. She told Chen that both her other men had finally died, and how she had sold the farm for a pittance. How she had made her long journey to this island in despair. He already knew from the servant that she had travelled more than five hundred *li*, all the way by junk from the estuary of the great Pearl River, south of Guangdong, with the coffin of her other son. He knew that the ferryman had, halfway across to the island, doubled the price of the passage claiming extra for the risk of bad luck from carrying the corpse. She had been forced to pay an extra twenty *taels*, or would have been thrown overboard.

She looked up at him directly for the first time and he saw the complete absence of fear in her. *"Ngo m-gau cheen* - I haven't enough money for this." She held out a string of grimy dull copper coins, square-holed in the centre, "This is all I have left." She threw the coins onto the stone floor between them.

"And I have this." She grasped the white porcelain jar and held it up. "The blood of my dead son."

Chen caught her gaze and held it, saw her slight frown as she looked at the irises of his eyes. Then he saw her understanding, and could feel her thinking what many had said since his own addiction to opium had started to eat into him and ruin his health - *wolf's eyes*.

"So. You too." She tensed with sorrow and rage. "You too. And so young." She reached forward for her bowl of tea. "Such a waste. And after you have trained for so long in the mysteries of your calling. So sad to let it go to waste."

"I am a master at carving." Chen was surprised at his defensive reply. He must try to retain her respect.

She glanced over at the carving of the figurehead on the stone bench. She looked up at him over the rim of the bowl, measuring him, then slowly returned the bowl to the floor. He heard the invitation in her voice, "So sad to accomplish nothing before you die."

Opium would kill him too, he knew, just as it had killed her son and her husband. *"M-hai sup-fun gan-yiu-ge"*, He replied, "It is of no great importance." He had meant that her lack of money was not important, but as he spoke Chen realised that in his tone he had admitted his own resignation. Had admitted to himself that nothing that was left was very important. They had all offended, he had to confess. Had offended their obligation and responsibility for the continuity of life by ruining their health, by knowingly and deliberately hastening their own deaths. Sinking into helpless addiction, each had sinned against his own ancestors, breaking the basic moral law of Confucius, that each man was to carefully look after his body, that sacred and precious legacy, entrusted to him by his ancestors as their precious link with their own descendants. In this, he knew and was forced to admit, he and each other addict had connived with the foreigners who shipped in the drug to the islands of Lintin and Hong Kong nearby, connived with the smugglers who smuggled it over the coastline and up the rivers, connived with the corrupt Mandarins who connived with the shippers, the smugglers, pirates and pedlars, who allowed it to happen and grew unbelievably rich by it, connived with the Manchus who were too weak to stop it.

"What is it that you desire from me?" Looking at her, Chen knew that she understood perfectly well that he already knew what she had come for. He must be getting better at his job, he thought ruefully. His sensitivity was increasing by the minute. Such a pity there was no time left.

The woman caught her breath, raising her head slowly to look into the shadows of the ceiling, frowning, concentrating on the devils she saw there. She drew breath again, deeply. When she spoke, her voice shocked him with its raw force. In tones struck from unbearable pain, he could feel the lesions in her scarred soul, as girl, as woman, as lover, as mother, as betrayed, "Somewhere, I know that there is a power who will feel my pain, which will listen, who will understand, who will act. I can feel it. I feel this power. All around me, connected by a thread." She looked down again, then quickly up. She looked directly across at him, her hands clenched, the distance between them seeming to contract and expand with his concentration in the dim evening light. "Tell me it exists. Tell me that I am not insane."

Chen sat still, watching the aura of light around her strengthen and glow, becoming more dense. "You are not insane."

Her energy was tangible in the air. He felt its purity like a charge across the back of his fingers as he moved his hand to smooth the silk over his knees. Yin. The female energy, essence of coolness, dark, reflection, calm. The moon energy, energy of the pull and flow of tides and of water and of blood. It controlled all fertility and growth, the cycles of birth, life and death.

The stillness and power of the female, nurturing in essence but merciless when betrayed. Chen understood with blinding clarity how each death, each injury, any injury to seed, limb, body, mind or soul, tree, plant or child was a rupture of the natural law, a breaking of the female force of wholeness and wellness and a betrayal and a denigration of the mother which had conceived, grown, nurtured and loved the young. From each hurt, each deceit, each death, each thoughtless or brutal injury, something died and a scar was left. Chen stopped himself from imagining how many scars there must be.

"And it does exist." He finished.

"Yes. I can feel it. But. But," She glanced around the interior, "it is out of reach.... I cannot make a connection. Can you? Can you make the connection? Do you know what it is?"

He looked at the light surrounding her, startled by its intensity. And then he had an idea. He would beguile her and get rid of her and then get on with his work. He looked at the porcelain jar. A conjunction formed in his mind.

"It is already moving closer," He said, reaching for jumbled smatterings of folk-lore which floated in his memory. "It is coming to you and you will join with it. It is the Yin, one half of the whole universe. The Blue Dragon. But you must keep her at bay. Keep her away."

"Yes! I can feel its strength coming!" She turned to the door, as if expecting an entry. "No! Not yet!" Chen was surprised that he had shouted, had stood up. He moved across to her and walked through her shining cocoon of light. He held her wrists, feeling her deep pulses in each one.

They stood silently for a long time, Chen concentrating, fixed on the task of resisting and diluting the force with his own male energy, anxious at his weakness, being drawn in by the feminine essence at her core. He began to recite a passage from the Shu-i-ki, emphasising its rhythms as he spoke the words, in his mind's eye following the characters down the pages of the ancient text, "There are four shapes of *Ling*, a Spiritual Being. They are the Unicorn, Phoenix, Tortoise and the greatest, the Dragon. A water snake after five hundred years changes into a *Mao*, a *Mao* after one thousand years changes into a *lung* - a dragon with fish scales - then a lung after five hundred years becomes a *Moh-lung*, the horned dragon; after another one thousand years it becomes a *ying-lung*, the dragon with wings... a divinity of water and rain and wind... with the head of a camel, the horns of a stag, the eyes of a demon, ears of a cow..." Chen felt the woman relax, the words soothing her. Her energy subsided gradually. He murmured on, pleased that he could still remember the words by heart, the neck of a snake, the belly of a clam, the scales of a carp of which one hundred and seventeen are imbued with good influence and thirty-six of which have bad influence, for the dragon is both a preserver and a destroyer. Each time they rise from the waters, winds arise and rain comes down, their voice of thunder and their glare is that of the sun and moon...." He began to stroke her hair, gently to the rhythm of his reciting, calming himself and comforted by the power of his deception. He would embellish.

"The Blue Dragon, the Mother Goddess, has a straight nose without any undulating horn. She may appear in different shapes - as a fresh and lovely girl or as an old hag. Summon her with great care and only in the light of the night with ground jade, Yu ying, pearls and special herb mixtures as prescribed in the texts to effect a ceremonial connection between the worshipper and the spirit of the deities.... listen for the claw of five-talons for it is the first sound you will hear......"

She reached calm, her head resting lightly on his shoulder. He led her to his master's own seat and sat her very gently down on it. The woman held on to him, gripping the loose folds of his clothes, looking up into his face with her shining eyes, clear and wet with tears, "Now I know. Now that I know. I ask you, young Priest, to send a curse with them, to send my own spirit back with their ship and their guns," Her voice burnt slow with guttural fire, "to lie at rest and then be set free to destroy in their own land, as they have destroyed me and my family."

Chen stood still, waiting for the flow of her energy to ebb again, collecting himself and his thoughts in its wake. A cluster of thoughts. About his long training. About his opium habit. About his futility. About his death. The cluster of thoughts formed into a decision. He nodded. He would help her. There was no going back. *"Gum-yat lai-baai say.* Today's Thursday. In two days there will be a full moon and no cloud."

"Ngo douh jee. I know" she murmured, "That is why I came. I prayed that a devil-ship would be here."

"And you will need to choose a male carrier for the seed of vengeance which you plant. A family line of male descendants, father to son, son to father, father to son. And you will need to choose the generation and a time when the evil seed will take root and grow and when its shoots will break the soil."

"Can they be tormented as the time passes? I want them tormented. To inherit torment."

"If you choose."

"Then I choose the captain of that great ship lying out there with its cargo of death."

"And the time?"

She considered. "How long for them to grow rich and complacent with their power. How long for their civilisation to reach its peak?"

There was a rustle at the door. Alice Capper stood with her veil down. She saw the woman and Chen, but ran to the figurehead and stood looking up at the carved face.

"But you have made me beautiful!" She exclaimed. For the first time, he sensed she was smiling under her veil. Chen felt a warm glow of pride. But quickly, Alice checked herself, her face reddening. "I have forgotten the scriptures."

Chen felt tense, losing control, skewered between the two women. "Scriptures?"

"Exodus 20:2-6," Alice put her chin up, drawing strength from her belief, "It says that you shall not carve idols for yourselves in the shape of anything in the sky above or on the earth below or in the waters beneath the earth; you shall not bow down before them or worship them. For I, the Lord, your God, am a jealous God, inflicting punishment for their fathers' wickedness on the children of those who hate me, down to the third and fourth generation."

"The third and fourth generation?" He repeated it in Chinese.

The woman stood up, speaking breathlessly in an undertone. "Then I choose the fourth generation of the captain of the ship, the fourth generation of his foul *Yingwok* loins. And I choose the moment when that young man's own seed is full and ready. Fullest and ripest. Then let the shoots of destruction break the soil."

Alice had moved to the tray of paint and lacqueurs. "What colour will be my tiara?" She turned to Chen, ignoring the Hakka woman completely. "My crown of thorns. Can it be red?"

"It can be done." Chen turned to the Hakka woman and spoke in Chinese. "It can be done."

"I want his heart to break as mine has been broken."

"Without reprieve?" Chen looked at Alice, repeating in English, "Without reprieve?"

"I know only kindness can cure a broken heart."

"Then there must be a sacrifice. Kindness borne of sacrifice," He looked at Alice, "As your scriptures say."

In this, he was, and had to appear, the master. He had never before attempted such a task and was terrified at the risk of being presumptuous in the eyes of the gods. He could not say in truth that he was certain he could perform the task successfully. Chen smoothed the palm of his hand over his shaven head. He glanced down at the white bindings on his feet and pulled the long, loose folds of his dark silk jacket over his chest. He could make the necessary preparations in accordance with his texts and the teachings he had learned, but the outcome would depend on her, and on the burning desire for revenge which, he thought as he watched her, was probably the only thing keeping her alive. *"Daan-hai hou ngai-heem.* But it will be very dangerous." He muttered, finishing his thought aloud, without realising it.

She sat still, waiting.

"And I will need this." Chen reached for the white porcelain jar.

11

Magic

Chen stood straight and walked through a curtain into a separate chamber lit by two small oil lamps. Yellowed in the dim light, row after row of small jars on deep mahogany shelves reached from floor to the dark upper regions of the ceiling. The rich and deep earth pungency of a thousand herbs, culled from the highest ravines to the smallest riverbeds across the vast Chinese Empire and stored in this room for centuries, cloyed the still air with a tangible mustiness. He ran his fingers along a line of jars, loving the feel of the smooth cool porcelain, as always calmed by the ordered rows, the contents of each jar catalogued and labelled in exquisitely neat characters by a brush held by a long-dead hand.

Chen knew very well that he should have followed the proper procedure. Knew well that he should obtain the permission from the High Priest. And knew that in a normal case any use of the necessary substance would have entailed payment of many thousands of *taels*, and have been preceded by days of ceremony and chanting. Chen recalled how he had felt as a young apprentice, being first summoned by his master into the dark chamber of secret herbs, to be introduced to the magic art and science of Ophiomancy. Chen felt the disapproval of his tutor now, could almost see him in the shadows, and was not surprised when his hand shook slightly as he reached upwards for the jars on the higher shelves.

Breathing deeply and softly to aid his concentration, Chen reached for a special jar deep in a corner and took it down. He brushed off a glistening thick carpet of cobweb. He had never heard of this compound having been used. Grasping the cupola of the lid, he gently pulled it off and carefully took out a small close-lidded round porcelain pot, a dragon snaking its way in blue glaze around the outside. Prising the lid off, he found inside the pot a ball covered in pale wax.

Leaving the jar and pot on the shelf, he took the wax ball to the round circular stone table in the centre of the room and with one swift downward blow cracked the wax skin against the stone. Inside was a smaller ball, wrapped in soft waxed cloth paper, dark-brown with age. Delicately, he unwrapped it, peeling the shreds of paper away with his fingernails and then held up to the light a soft dark caked globe, minutely-speckled with shining lights reflecting from the lamps. He paused, turning the ball in the light, marvelling at what it contained. The soul substance of the Great Mother, the Moon Goddess, the Blue Dragon. The essence of Yin, the principle of darkness, cold and death. A priceless substance, made from a recipe now only known in mythical lore, from ingredients described only in the texts of legends. He raised the ball to his nostrils, surprised by the piquant fragrance of fresh summer blossom which had been preserved in the wax for centuries.

He knew he should at least perform some ceremony. Seek some payment. As he drew the curtain aside, Chen could hear his tutor's voice give a shocked and despairing reprimand. By this action he would shame his tutor, he knew, and he would pay dearly for it when he died, when his *Chi*, the living breath energy, became *Shen ming* and tried to rise on wings to the Sky Paradise. "Magic depends on Order," his master had told him, many times, "and the correct sequence of chanting and ceremony, the correct words, the correct actions, the correct thoughts, all in the proper Order. Order reflects the Order of the Universe and the Heavens, the Order of the Gods. Without Order, the players in the game cannot have the right sensitivities, the correct actions, they will not know when the time has come for a conjunction of forces. Without Order there will be mistakes."

But there could be no ceremony. The woman had no money for decorations, charcoal fires, candles and oil-lamps to be kept tended, the joss and herbs to be burnt, the chanting priests, special readings from the texts. Chen had decided to proceed. They would do it alone and together. From his heart, he cast a silent apology over his shoulder to his tutor's spirit, and walked through the curtain.

Returning to the woman in the main chamber, he held the ball out to her. "You must eat nothing except for this, until it is over. It will make you strong."

Handing the cake to her, he wondered how much, if anything, he should explain so that she might know the processes which she was about to invoke. And the power she was to let loose. Should he tell her of the Yellow Dragon riding in the moonlight on rippling water, unseen and unknown, whose kin's soul-substance she was now eating in the crushed pearl and ten-thousand-year-old jade-grease crystals embedded in the cake? Of the *hu fun lei*, the dragon-tears, sap from the weeping-tree, mixed up with it? That, once eaten, it would attune her mind with an unbearable sensitivity to form a direct connection with the Mother Goddess and that because of the mind-strengthening power of the huchu herb, she would be prevented from feeling any hunger, thirst, cold and fatigue - but only for a time, whilst her body collapsed beneath her?

Chen wryly glanced up at the characters written in red and gold down the sides of the door to the herb-room, the first a fragment from a poem, "If we do not seek the dragons, They also will not seek us". On the other side of the door, the second was a quotation from Confucius, "Respect the spirits," said Confucius, "and keep them at a distance."

Practical reminders.

It was her choice. She sought the Blue Dragon, controller of wind and water, the Great Mother of the East, and he would try to make the link, as she had asked, through the Pearl of Heaven. He would let her find it.

When she had finished the cake, Chen called his servant and told him to go home. Then Chen moved into the central chamber and unlocked the *Knei Pi*, the ancient seven-circled jade dagger - seven circles engraved in the large circle between haft and blade, perfectly balanced in his hand - to be used only in sacrifices to the sun, to the stars and to the Goddess of the Moon. There was no record in the texts of it ever having been used. As far as Chen knew, the jade knife had not been unlocked in living memory.

12

Lodgement

The Captain and all of the crew were anxious at the delay. But when the heavy figurehead, freshly painted and lacquered, was finally rowed out to the Sea Witch in thick sack-cloth and slowly and carefully winched up on pulley-blocks to its position and Joe and the other carpenter had drilled and pinioned it in position at the prow, all stood back with pride at her fearless beauty, her red crown of thorns glinting sharply in the sunlight.

Curiously, everyone on board now began to treat Alice Capper with respectful awe. Unfortunately, this had not prevented Captain Doe from docking a third of Chen's fee for the delay in delivering the figurehead to the ship on the pretext that the delay had caused expensive additional provisioning. Looking up at the full moon, the Captain had just finished congratulating himself with a glass of port when a flash of spiralling lightning split the dark sky, and a dissonant deep drum rumbled a reverberation across the bay. The captain dropped his glass and dived below.

In the stillness, the dying candles flickered. Everyone on deck felt the beginning of the wind and raised their eyes to look up at the fingers of cloud swarming suddenly upwards, reaching for the moon.

"*Hai-yaaaaah...Hai-yaaaaah!*" The scream had come from the front of the boat, right by the prow.

Joe followed three armed sailors and several Chinese as they rushed along the deck to the prow. There, two Chinese were calling and waving, pointing over the high rail down at the water beneath the figurehead. They all clustered tight against the rail looking downwards.

Far beneath them, the silhouette of the small sampan stood out clear and flat against the oily intensity of the yellow moon-track on the water. Candles had been lit, placed all around the box in the middle of the small boat. In the prow sat a Chinese woman, upright and erect. In the stern, a figure swathed in thick silks tended an open charcoal brazier, his shaved head shining in the glow, his eyes in shadow. As Joe looked down, Chen drew out from the folds of his clothing a small red bag and poured the contents onto the fire. In seconds, a mephitic vaporous stink slid into the nostrils of all who watched from the ship. A smell of rotten honeysuckle and almonds.

Nobody on the ship moved or spoke as the intrusive vapour crept into their minds. An officer standing next to Joseph had cleared his throat and had begun to move, but the spectacle overcame them all. A stillness entered the scene. A solemn stillness, in which light and dark grew more intense, shade grew and receded. The wavemounds undulated in the harsh moonlight, sinuous rungs of a ladder from the moon, crossed by a trellis of silver.

Chen began to chant, a pulsing rhythm, and they saw him empty another red bag in the fire. The woman stood and slowly raised her eyes to them. Each man looking down felt that she was looking up directly at him. Her stillness held them, her gaze held them all. Each man felt an open channel of energy flow between him and those eyes. Was it the moonlight or were they all aware of her beauty, as the lines of her cheekbones softened, and the still gaze held them?

She slowly raised both arms. In her hands she held high above her head a shining green dagger with a large circle between hilt and blade. She waited, perfectly still, the sampan moving gently in the swell. All waited, locked with her in that long fragment of time, not knowing what it was that they awaited, but sensing somehow that they were helpless as they did. They became aware of a new sound, heard behind the drone-chant of the priest and the noise of the cicadas. Or was it the sound of the cicadas that had altered? A subtle modulation, distant but approaching, the sound of a claw on close rungs of a trellis. From above them. From the horizon. From the sky. From the moon.

The woman began to moan, a deep wheezing moan from her chest, which raised slowly in pitch to a howl, lasting until her breath was completely spent. She snapped her head back, looking up into the sky, searching the clouds. Then she gave a cry of recognition and plunged the dagger into her chest, her eyes bulging out, fixed on the sky above her. The gaze of each man on the ship was wrenched upward. There, formed in the swirling clouds, its fronds and snake scales etched by the moon in silver, a dragon head looked down at them, its tail whipping the clouds like a huge angry cat. Five razor talons split the light and tore at the solid cloud masses. A crack of thunder. Two long slow streams of lightning snaked down from its eyes, in cold blue irradiating electric ribbons. The tips of the high-voltage charges fell in two places, only yards apart, both at the same time. One reached into the small sampan, to the circle at the centre of the protruding dagger, snaked to the metal of the brazier, exploded and the sampan began to blaze furiously.

The other sheet of lightning connected, fleetingly, with a metal pin holding a wire support stay on the top of the figurehead of the ship. For a moment, the glossy lacqueured blood paint of the Sea Witch's carved oaken thorns, her face, head and flowing hair were cossetted and suffused with spectral blue-white-blue static mist.

13

After the flaming carcass of the sampan had been fended off with poles and had drifted out to sea to sink, long after the human hubbub had died, long after the noise on the ship had finished and the silence had swollen, Novice Chen had not tried to swim to the shore, or even to move. He still floated in the dark water, face up, his arms outstretched. He found that by breathing evenly and regularly, the scorching burns on his hands and arms would hurt less and that he could float easily in the cool, heavy salt water, soothed by its rhythms. He gazed up at the sleekness of the Sea Witch, the long sensual curve of her lines, the gold lettering high above him, dimly seen, his eyes drawn to the face of the figurehead.

Maybe he was still in extreme shock, maybe it was the numbing cold of the night water, maybe worsened by opium withdrawal. But he no longer wondered if it had all been a mistake, simply an odd cloud-formation that had happened to appear like the dragon with a coincidental electric storm. Whether the woman had killed herself for nothing. He felt humbled by what had happened. He had been given divine confirmation of the unspeakable. By this, the truth could now occur to him, with a gentle smile, that he had never really believed in the legends and that he really had not known what to expect.

He felt that he had been fulfilled. Lulled by the silence, quiescent as he floated, he felt his energy sapped and his life ebb, sleep creeping in. As he let his breath slowly out of his body and felt the water gently encroach, salt in his mouth, he looked up one last time at the figurehead far above him, watched her fly in the dark, her eyes gaze out to the horizon and to the future. Beneath the red crown, the hard chiselled lines of the wooden face softened, her eyes looked down at him in the water. He watched her lips begin to move. Sinking into the water's welcome, as it closed over his face, he heard her soft voice clearly in his ears, her sussuration fill his mind, as she whispered to him not to worry, not to worry, his task had been fulfilled, that he had fulfilled his duty to the woman, and that sure enough, sure enough in time, her revenge would finally come.

"An act of kindness is an antidote to evil in this world." Alice Capper's words came to him from nowhere. The wooden features had softened again. "Only kindness can cure a broken heart. But there must be a sacrifice."

The very last thoughts of Novice Chen were a memory and a guess, threaded like beads on a rope in his mind. In the thick darkness of the water, the voice of the figurehead sang in his memory as his body slowly turned and sank. How similar but how different the voice of the woman had been to the voice which he had just heard. The guess merged into the understanding and the understanding became a certainty just as he died in the water. The three spirits, the spirit of the woman, the spirit of the ship and the spirit of the Great Moon Goddess had combined and merged into a new, fragile, vengeful, raw, tempestuous, powerful and merciless being. A being which held in it all the spirit power of wood, wind and sea, and of the human and of the elemental. It had spoken to him. And he was certain that it now lived in and filled its own beautiful shape at the prow of the ship.

PART SIX

14

Jane Tench

Ventnor was a bit eerie at 5 in the morning. I could hear seagulls down on the Esplanade, but no other sound. The streets were empty. Tourists gone, the town had closed in on itself for the winter. It felt forgotten. Daylight, when it came, showed just the supermarket, a few charity shops and some early estate agents gazing hopelessly at their computers. But that was what I loved about it – the feeling of isolation. It was why I had come here in the first place. It had, of course, been deliberate career suicide. I won't bore you with the small print of my relationships, basically because there hadn't been any to speak of. As to background, well, not much really. My parents were of Irish stock and ran a smallholding midway between Matamata and Morrinsville, south of Auckland. Our family went back generations, lost in the mists of time and seasons. To me, it was suffocating.

I had left my parents in New Zealand and qualified as a narrative therapist in the hope that by listening I could get close to people. No, that's actually not true. If I am honest, I had had to get away and had really qualified because the discipline was not particularly difficult and in order to gain respect from people with problems, people who needed help. They looked up to me. It made me safe, put me above them, safe and protected by the mystique of expertise, the illusion of care.

Some began to cloy, to be honest. Their gratitude sometimes developed into a rather sickly admiration. Fawning. And then I made a mistake. In London I had an affair with a patient. Totally unprofessional, of course. It was flattering and fun at first and I enjoyed the power I had over him. But I quickly twigged that it was driven by his need, not mine, and I soon felt swamped. Then I found out he was a drug dealer. Unlike most successful drug dealers, he was also an addict.

Confronting him, watching him squirm, I finally had to face something that had always been there. I didn't actually like people that much. They quickly bored me. Someone once said that if you know a person's story you can't dislike them. Trouble was, I didn't really want to know their stories. Truth is, I ran away, kidding myself that I could make a living on the Isle of Wight, but really following my gut into a place where I thought I could escape. In the end I just wanted to be alone. And then I found out that he had made a video of us having sex and had posted it on the web. The legal fees for getting it taken down had basically bankrupted me and I was certain it was still on some websites. Paranoid, I wore dark glasses, a hat and a scarf for months afterwards.

I stared at my reflection in the bathroom mirror. I could see why people thought me attractive – dark brown hair, good bone structure, light blue eyes, full lips, good body. The surface things were OK and I had, of course, used them to gain employment, given my thin experience. But after the affair I had been asked to leave, thankfully without any difficult record being made. Thanks partly, no, in truth wholly, because I had shopped him as a drug-pusher to the police and my testimony had done for him. Client confidentiality had nothing to do with it. I had to get rid of him. My career was at stake and I had needed to survive. Driscoll must know. But then he wouldn't care about that. He was palming me off as a tick in a box to save his fat arse.

My career had been a mess. I was a charlatan. Worse, I knew my ex would come for me as soon as he was released from jail. Soon. I had to stay low, make some money, disappear.

Now, I realised that the dynamic had changed. Adam Doe frightened me. My first instinct on waking up was to go call Driscoll and cancel my contract as soon as his office opened. Tear it up and forget about it. I was out of my depth.

A dilemma. Fake it and go for the cash as long as possible or give up and slide into local jobs. Problem was, the tourist season was over and menial tasks were non-existent and I really couldn't see myself working as a waitress alongside the hapless Fiona.

The flat door opened and Fiona came in, clutching an envelope. She looked pale and tired.

"Post for you." She handed me the large brown envelope and slumped on the sofa. "The Food Bank's on Wednesday. Anything left to eat?"

I decided that I had to get rid of Fiona. I opened the envelope without replying. It was from Driscoll. There were the formal papers but no advance payment. I looked down at Fiona, now asleep. No money equals Fiona. No

Fiona requires money. The envelope, I felt, was a beckoning finger. I had to go further. I had no choice.

15

Capper's Gorge

Adam Doe's grandmother had sounded resigned on the 'phone, as if she had given up all hope. But she would see me.

I walked the mile of the flat concrete embankment sea defences between Ventnor and Monks Bay, then the track upwards. The track fell a few yards, bent sharply by some old stables under thick sycamore trees and ended, cut off at the very edge of the cliff, its hardcore foundations indecently exposed to the English Channel wide and flat before me. Sunlight gilded the highest leaves and yellowed the high twisted chimneys on the stables. A pigeon warbled away and a plume of blue smoke rose against a line of deep green trees to the east. A sign in faded red and white warned that the cliff path had fallen away. Slung from a post, a hand-painted board indicated a new cliff path higher up, through a new hole in a very old wall and the waving dry grasses of a field beyond.

I passed the red and white sign and was pleased to find that it lied. There was a steep path down to the beach, twisting amongst mighty slabs of dried fallen clay, already overgrown. Halfway down, another rusty signpost which had once been ornate protruded at an angle from a slab of clay, forlornly pointing a solitary finger at the sky. Perched on the rim of the sea, a white steamer made its sturdy passage up the Channel. At the end of the steep path, I saw the slate-roof of a tiny flint building shrunk in deep against the bottom of the cliff. Behind it and along, the cliff rose high and sharp as a layered cake freshly cut, crumbs of rock and fallen clay piled up at its foot, the sea like a flat plate, wide and golden green, its surface mottled with long purple cloud shadows.

In the next cove was a small stone quay with a cluster of boats drawn up on the slipways. A row of substantial Edwardian houses in bright colours were stacked up on the quay. A tractor was pulling a fishing boat out of the water and a few late holiday-makers stood about watching.

Above me, dense woodland stretched upward all across the looming immensity of the downs to the very peak, the tips of the trees silvered by the early afternoon sun. I could just make out the tips of groups of yellow stone chimneys, disclosing the hiding places of large houses, sunk deep in the trees.

There was an orchard, the apple trees in dishevelled rows, hunched and spreading their limbs inland, as if terrified of losing their grip in the next storm. I picked a small early apple and munched it. The sunny calm did feel strange to me - the place did have a magical sort of atmosphere, but to me it suggested that everything that was magic had happened a long time ago - that nothing would happen now in a world of cars, the internet, political correctness and brightly clothed holiday makers - that the magic was hidden and was asleep, waiting for another time to show itself. I followed the path round the headland to Capper's Gorge.

16

Lucretia Doe

I had left the file and papers in the flat on purpose. I knew that there was a danger in looking too official, too investigative. As I knocked on the door, I noticed that the tiny cottage was well-kept, the garden with a patch of mown lawn bordered with bright flowers, the names of which I didn't know. The sun was very bright, with a cold, clean wind shrieking in under the eaves from the east. The wind had backed from the south-west and now pushed against the tide, dark-green mounds of waves rolling in from the Atlantic Ocean across the great stretch of English Channel, punctured momentarily by the spikes of the outer rocks then lunging and spuming up dark and grey, thumping on the shore.

Today, everything was solid, bright and real. The keen brightness of the morning brought a new feeling of confidence and a fresh clarity. It was all nonsense, I thought. My imagination had run away with me. It was all ridiculous. I was safe. I decided to listen to Adam Doe, patiently help him out over as long as possible, collect Driscoll's money then forget about it. Once I had the money, I could do as I liked.

Lucretia Doe was the chatty type. Not resentful in the least at my visit. She was obviously grateful I had come.

"Miss Tench welcome!" She opened the door with a big smile and offered me breakfast. "Mister Driscoll telephoned to tell me you were coming." She busied about the tiny kitchen, pinned back an errant tress of grey hair and fussed about in her baggy flowered dress, cooking a delicious mound of bacon, sausages, eggs, tomatoes, toast and mushrooms. Wonderful free food.

"Adam has gone out but will be back shortly, Miss Tench."

"Jane, please. Call me Jane." I managed this through a mouthful.

"Well, Jane, most people call me Luke and you can too. I sent Adam out for a bit because I really wanted to have a quiet word with you first." She looked up at me, "A little bit of background, if you like." She had beautiful eyes – intelligence beneath kindness. She must have been a real stunner when she was younger.

Luke told me she had lived alone since her husband died. Adam was her only grandson. Adam's parents were divorced and Adam had come down to the Island to stay with her for a few weeks and had stayed for over a year. Then the problems suddenly started.

"Nobody knows what happened to him and he won't say a word. He just writes these stories. Won't talk about it. From Mister Driscoll, we've had one help after another, all pretty useless."

"What happened to him? I mean, what triggered the problems? Was there a specific event, a turning point?"

Luke tensed her shoulders, a finger lifted to straighten her hair, took a deep breath, "The police were good about it, kept it out of the County Press." She rallied, her voice on automatic, telling the facts which she must have repeated time and time again.

"He was found in the cellar of this house, covered in mud, in shock. He had PTSD, post-traumatic stress disorder. Months of flashbacks, nightmares, pain, sweating, feeling sick, trembling." She was finding it difficult reminding herself.

"I really couldn't cope with it. He had withdrawn into himself," She shrugged, "and there was the opium."

"What?"

"He was found with a lot of opium. He had been taking it, in bigger doses. I hadn't a clue. When I found it, big balls of it, I called the hospital and they called the police."

"Is he off it now?"

"I think, hope, so. I can't actually be sure. He won't talk to me, see. I don't know where he got it from." She turned towards the window. "They didn't know either. It was very strange, the whole thing. They decided not to prosecute as long as he went for psychotherapy. Mr. Driscoll has done his best, poor mite. But nobody could figure it out, the source, I mean."

"The source?" This was all getting a bit close.

"The police sent it to forensics, who did a test on it." Luke turned to face me, throwing the line away as if she had tired of the whole thing, suddenly looking exhausted.

"They found out that the opium was over 150 years old."

17

Luke pulled out some wellington boots and a big old fisherman's mackintosh and insisted that I put them on and walk with her along the sand. "Fresh air", she said. "We'll collect some driftwood for the fire." She grabbed an old wicker basket.

My stomach full, misgivings started to fade. I was actually beginning to like Luke. She was matter-of-fact, uncomplicated, kind.

Against the wind, we staggered down the cliff-path and reached the Boathouse on the shore. "I've brought the key, you can look inside later," She took my arm and together we bent across the beach, picking up scraps of driftwood, the freezing spray whipping up from the shingle and stinging our faces.

"What did your husband do, Luke?"

"He was the pier-master at Ventnor, just like his father before him. Before it fell into the sea and was demolished. He always wanted to go to sea but....," She shrugged, "I wouldn't let him. I told him I would always worry that he wouldn't come back. Well, he understood and settled for the closest he could get. He always said that if I wanted him to stay at home, at least he could be on the sea at the end of the long wooden plank. That's what he called it, the pier - 'The long wooden plank'. He had a tremendous sense of fun, the total opposite to his own father, who had no sense of fun at all and was mortally terrified of the sea!"

"Adam's great-grandfather?"

"Mmh. Nobody could ever understand it, even his wife, and the local doctors knew nothing of mental illness in those days. He was even afraid of the sound of the sea. He hated living here, but couldn't tear himself away. He was fascinated and horrified at the same time. He insisted on staying on as Master of the Pier. It must have been terrifying for his poor wife, like a compulsion - an addiction which she could see was destroying him, torturing his nerves." She shuddered. "My husband said that his own mother had told him much later - a long time after Adam's great-grandfather disappeared - that at the time of a full moon he would stay on at the end of the pier throughout the night. He would creep home in the early light, brooding and silent. Before he finally disappeared, he confided to her in a lucid moment that he had been listening to a voice from the sea, telling him stories. He said that the voice was beautiful, but was full of malice. It held him in cringing awe and eventually drove him craven mad, poor tormented devil," She paused.

"Where did he go to when he disappeared....?"

"Well, nobody knows for certain. Afterwards, they found that a scow with a small sail had been cast off, missing from the end of the pier. Or he might have thrown himself into the water. Nobody knows. His body was never found and no-one ever saw him again.... drawn off the end of the pier by the voice from the sea." Luke finished wistfully.

"Could it be hereditary? With Adam, I mean."

She stopped and sat down on a rock. Looked out to sea across the waves. "Something else has happened to him. He's changed. Gone inside himself."

"Luke. I've read his story. The first part. Driscoll gave me photocopies of the whole thing. I need to speak to him. Find out if it means anything."

She looked at me, "The change was so sudden. If I didn't know better, Jane, I would say it was love sickness. But then we found the drugs. Hopelessness. The type that makes you want to die. We've tried everything. I'm too old to look after him, but he's got nowhere else to go."

She got up and took my arm, leaning in confidentially, "He keeps this old photo with him, won't let go of it. Some school children. He takes it out and gazes at it. Sometimes he cries."

We walked out into the wind, collecting bits of dry driftwood. As we passed the Boathouse, the big double-doors, which clearly had been put in recently, were wide open. Almost filling the centre of the tiny space was a sharp-prowed mahogany carvel dinghy, its varnish thick with dust. Inside, two men were sorting tackle up on an old wooden platform, which resembled a large sort of bunk.

"Not going sailing today then, Lucretia?" One called, laughing. Luke introduced them to me. Jack and his son. They ran the crab restaurant in Horseshoe Bay and she explained that she let them use the boathouse for storing nets and pots. Jack came down from the platform, running his hand along the edge of the boat as he came forward to shake my hand, "So this is your grandson's little helper, eh?" He looked at me closely and then turned back to the boat, "She grows more beautiful with age, just like you, Lucretia." They all laughed. "My offer still stands, you know." He said more seriously, gazing at her.

"Which one of the offers, Jack? To buy the boat or to marry me?" She met his gaze, smiling at him fondly, without coquettishness.

"Both! Of course, both still stand! But I was talking of the boat. I know you'll never take up the other offer, Lucretia, I'm not young anymore," He said, laughing, "But the boat, if you sell her to me I'll sail her round to Horseshoe today, even in this weather!"

"No Jack. I'll never sell her, you know that and you understand the reason. Anyway, I'm sure that Adam will want to use it while he stays with me. When the weather improves and so on. Fresh air might do him some good." She looked at me, "Why don't you stay here while I take the wood up?" She grinned at Jack as she left, "Jack here can sometimes be quite interesting, as long as he's not asking you to marry him!"

"Absolutely right on! Dead right!" A young man bounced through the door in an orange shirt and bright-green trousers. No dress sense, then. Distracted, mind on other things or just colour blind?

"Hi guys!" He nodded to the men and then came and stood by me, carefully avoiding the dirty boat and tackle, "I was up on the cliff and I saw you two coming in here. When are you coming over? I came to find you," He touched my arm, "Can I use your old jacket to sit down on?"

"Adam, this is Jane Tench."

"Hi." A low voice. No pleasantries, no introduction. The vigour of his entrance suddenly went. He closed his eyes, dropped his shoulders. I had to admire his strategy. He had waited for me to be hemmed in by company on neutral ground, wanting to sound me out before I could get him alone, but the weight of his obvious depression had dropped on him. I was off-footed. Adam Doe was not what I had expected at all. He was good-looking, tall, slim, well-muscled, tousled auburn hair. I saw Luke's intelligent eyes without the kindness. Arrogant, I felt. Challenging. A survivor. His troubles disguised as best he could.

"We'll talk later." I murmured. As I reluctantly took my jacket off and laid it on the floor, the younger man, Jack's son, came down the rickety ladder from the platform and took out a flask of hot tea. The two men sat on sacking on the hard earth floor and the younger poured tea into two plastic cups, passed one to Jack and one to me, "Here, you finish this first, there's plenty - there's no running water down here, so I can't wash it up."

"Thanks very much." I said, sipping away.

"I'll have to learn to row and to sail before I can use the boat." Flat voice. Something to say. Adam Doe was watching me carefully.

Jack tried his best to lighten the atmosphere, talking too much to avoid silence, "What, you're Luke's grandson and you can't sail? Your grandfather would turn in his grave if he could hear you! Well then, we'll have to teach you to sail. When the wind goes round to the west or south-west, which it won't for a bit. There's a big storm coming in from the east, from Northern Europe - we won't go out - even though without the crabs our restaurant business suffers. The sea's just too dangerous with the wind in this direction."

"Partic'ly across the shoal of big rocks 'n out from the bay," Said the younger man, his voice rolling in the south-Wight accent, "A lethal spot that."

"Where the *Sea Witch* went down," Interjected the older man, turning to Adam, "You must have heard about that, being Luke's grandson!"

Adam was looking at me, "No, no I haven't." He drew his hand up to his mouth, still looking at me, playing a game, "What happened to the...., the..."

"The Sea Witch."

"Sea Witch. The Sea Witch." As I said the name, without any warning at all, I felt a spark of excitement crawl up my spine and reach the back of my neck. From the dark recesses, caught at the edge of my mind's eye, a curious picture had quickly come and disappeared before I had time to look at it, a premonition - of a curtain beginning to twitch as a finger behind it felt to draw it back. I leant towards the man, "What happened to her?"

117

Of course I had read the story, but it would be useful to hear another version. For some reason, my mouth felt dry. I drank more tea.

"It's a sad tale," The man Jack took a sip from the cup and settled deeper on his sacking, his voice thickening, "The Sea Witch was quite simply the fastest and most beautiful clipper ever. She was built here on the island at Daniel List's yard in Fishbourne at Wootton Creek," He waved his arm towards the back wall, "No expense was spared. Amongst seafarers she was a legend, a true thoroughbred from truck to keel. Faster and more powerful than any other sailing ship anywhere, before or since - and that includes the *Cutty Sark,* the *Arrow, The Falcon,* faster than any of them. Nothing could match her, although many tried."

"What happened to her?"

"Opium." Jack pronounced the word with disgust, "She was sold - to one of the Hongs."

I had never heard the word before. Seeing my perplexity, Jack explained. *"Hongs.* It's a Chinese word they used for the British traders when they set up in Hong Kong in the nineteenth century, grew rich from smuggling opium drugs into China. They shipped from India to China, off-loaded the opium into smaller craft and then secretly carried it up the river arteries of China, and killed millions of 'em in the process...."

The doors banged suddenly as the wind caught them. Jack's son got up and shut them, taking back the cup from me as he passed. He sat back against the sacking, waiting for Jack to continue.

"The Sea-Witch was always the first with the new crop. Too fast for the Chinese pirates, even in a typhoon. When she came home, laden with the spoils of the deadly trade, case upon case of silver dollars and treasures, she regularly made the journey across the world back to the pilot at Gravesend in eighty-four days flat...."

"The normal passage took one hundred and twenty odd days, to give you some idea," Put in the younger, "She shaved nearly forty days' sailing off the run."

Jack looked irritated at the interruption, he was savouring the story as he told it. He would have been boring if there hadn't been an unseen electric current running between Adam and me as we listened.

"Especially when you think that she had a tonnage of 850 tons and was more than two hundred feet from stern to figurehead. She could do twenty knots through the sea, with a full suit of racing sails and spars."

Adam stood up, yawning. "Look, I'll see you later." He put his hand on my arm, "I suppose you can come over to the house when you're through with this...O.K.?" He delivered it as a command, not waiting for a reply. I nodded, groundwork was being offered, contact established with the Client, progress made.

Adam made for the doors, then suddenly changed his mind and wandered behind the dinghy and into the back of the boathouse. We could hear him poking about in the piles of junk in the far corner.

"850 tons at 20 miles an hour!" Jack was obviously obsessed with the story, "Magnificence made alive...." He was obviously not going to stop and I began to understand why Luke didn't want to marry him. "Her

119

woodwork comparable to the work of a first-class cabinetmaker. Her rails, stanchions, sky-lights and binnacles must have dazzled with gleaming brasswork, not a curve or line or an angle which didn't suggest perfection, she had a look of delicate - almost fragile - beauty...."

There was a pause, only the occasional boom of the wind and rattle from the window-frame interrupting Jack's silent reverie. After a bit, the younger man stood up and walked to the window, peering down at the sea seething over the shoal, "When she hit those rocks over there, it marked the end of an era. An era we'll never see again."

They both ruminated. After a while, to break the silence, now anxious to leave and make progress with Adam, I asked "So, if The Sea Witch was so wonderful why didn't they build another one?"

Both men laughed. "Good question! But it wasn't that easy in those days. Unless you had very detailed plans, you couldn't get close! And even then you could find you'd built a different ship! It all relied on the instinct and genius of the one man - the designer -who would check every detail as the ship was built, from the trees cut and bent for the keel to the rope used for the rigging and the canvas in the sails. It was truly an art, an art now long lost. Nobody had kept the plans and the designer refused, when he learnt about the opium. They offered him a fortune, enough to buy up half of this island lock, stock and barrel. But he still wouldn't do it. He died shortly after."

"Many died in the wreck, too," Said the younger man, "Most washed away. When the Captain was eventually got ashore, he was well enough but didn't last long. The legend says he loved the Sea Witch beyond any woman."

It sounded exotic, like a fairy tale, as of course I well knew.

"But how do you know about all this, all this detail?" I kept my voice flat, carefully aware that Adam was still within ear-shot.

Jack wiped his hands on the back of his overalls, looking across at me. "Because of the books," He said, walking past the boat into the gloom at the back of the room, where Adam was standing with a pair of sticks in his hand, turning them in the dim light. Jack ignored him and bent down and pulled open the lid of a rusting tin box, "The ships logs, all of them, are in here - and they'll make your hair stand on end when you read them - every captain's account of the passages of the Sea Witch across the world from when she was built to when she went down, out on those rocks over there - only about fifteen land miles away from where she was first launched."

He reached in and brought out a stained leather-bound book, opened it and rested it against the gunwhale of the dinghy, turning the stiff pages. Finding the page he wanted, he waved me over, "This is a note written in ink by the last captain, the night before she hit those rocks out there. The logs are thankfully still legible." He began to read aloud and I glanced at Adam, knowing that I was going to have to sit through another long speech about stanchions and things like that. Still, I had to be polite.

Jack was Luke's friend. Luke was the key to Adam. So I stood and listened, clenching my jaw to stop yawning.

But then, as Jack read, a strange thing happened. As I listened to the written words, all the years seemed to roll away, as if we were hearing the voice of the captain standing in front of us "..... 23rd September – 12.05 a.m. barometer 25.39 falling. Wind strengthening to more than gale-force from S.S.E. Ebb tide. High-running sea. Thick, gloomy weather. Again, called all hands, further reefed the mainsail. Increasing ugly head-sea. All small sails in, and fore and mizzen topgallants. Watch on look out for Isle of Wight to North ..."

Jack paused, "Those were the facts as she sailed in towards the island, but he didn't know what was waiting for him. So he carried on writing."

Adam was watching me furtively, waiting for me to react. I kept my expression bland. So this was where he had got it all from, I realised. His story was all a fake, taken from the Captain, his ancestor. My job had suddenly come to an end. For how long could I string this out with Driscoll now that I knew?

Jack continued reading:

"Saint Catherine's Light sighted, South of Wight, 12.30 a.m. Being nearly at the finish of our voyage I record here that it has been during my present passage in the Sea Witch round Good Hope from the Orient that I have learnt to comprehend and to adopt a singular and unearthly belief that prevails, and will always prevail, among seamen; and it is in her, and by her, that I am first touched by that strange sympathy which is created by a favourite, by an outstanding ship, upon the minds of an appreciative crew. If the Sea Witch was a living being, that sympathy could scarcely be greater. She resents every neglect in her handling, and rebels at once against any over-pressure or any tampering with her trim, so that our common expressions – used by me, my officers and crew alike, that could have no meaning to a landsman – that she is complaining or sulking or offended, seem to us to be rightfully applied …. "

The doors suddenly opened and Luke entered with a cold gust of wind, "Lunch is……" Her voice trailed away as she saw the three of us, Jack standing like a preacher holding the book, the other two of us sitting, faces raised to him as he read, in rapt attention. Seeing the book, she paled. But then she quietly nodded across to Jack and came to sit next to me on my coat. Jack looked down at the younger man and then at me and Luke sitting together on the floor. We all waited in silence for Jack to continue reading the words of the long-dead captain.

"I have learnt to look upon her as a thing completely alive, to be loved and petted. As they say, she can do everything but speak."

Jack glanced up from the book quickly at Lucretia and then continued reading the captain's words, "but I confess, knowing in truth that this log is not the proper place for these thoughts, that there are times when alone under a bright moon on her quarterdeck, admiring her exquisite grace under a fair wind, I feel that I can hear her voice murmuring softly of her pleasure, whispering in the soft rush of her bow through the water…."

Jack finished. Leaving the book open at the page he had read, he came forward and put it in my hands. I took it in silence, my throat aching with sadness at what I had just heard.

"They say that after he was got ashore after the wreck, he sent for his wife and son. But before they arrived, he had died, they say of a broken heart."

Jack took a noisy gulp of cold tea. "Although the details are almost completely forgotten now, those who know anything about it at all know, for certain, that the shame of the people of this shore will never be forgiven. Lucretia knows it. Murder and greed, although they say that half of the gold and the silver was never found." Beneath his thick brows, his eyes looked suddenly up at Adam, almost accusingly, "And you should know and remember it too."

I felt a chill, the dark curtain in my mind drawing further aside. I stood up. I was aware that Lucretia had also risen and that the other man had turned from the window and that they were all watching Adam solemnly.

Suddenly, incongruously, Adam started beating the sticks on the top of the tin chest, the deep muffled drum roll echoing slightly from the stone walls.

"It's in your blood, lad." The men stood silently, watching Adam's face. The wind growled. With a frightened glance at me, Lucretia went to Adam and held onto his hand tightly, "Jack, I really don't think that Adam is ready for this yet...."

But Jack ignored her, caught up in his story. "Ask Lucretia about the wrecking. About the shame. And about the captain. A part of him lives in you now....," he chuckled grimly, "and more than like, a part of the Sea-Witch as well..."

I swivelled to look at Lucretia, "When did all this happen?" I felt rising panic, but couldn't understand why, "Why is the captain inside of him? When did all this happen? Why him?"

"1849" The two men said it in unison as if having waited for my question. Lucretia had not spoken. They kept on looking at Adam. The older man glanced an enquiry at Lucretia. I sensed that she had hesitated before she nodded back to Jack in answer to the glance, giving her consent. Then, speaking quietly but very clearly as if before an audience, as if throwing down a challenge, Jack looked across at Adam. "The last captain." He paused. "Captain Doe. He was your great-great-grandfather. Your grandpa's grandad. Go and see, in the graveyard, where he lies with the Sea Witch herself!"

As Luke waited for the two men to pack up their things and emerge, I stood outside in the shelter of the wall, looking down at the thin faded handwriting on the page. Each line started in immaculate copperplate but then ended at all angles. I could almost feel the hurling motion of the ship, could hear the timbers creaking in the cabin, as I read the very last entry in the log, the words that Jack had not read out....

"1.00 am. Same weather, growing worse still. Distress flare sighted close to cliffs under St. Boniface with dim lights. Hove to. Sent up rockets and burned blue lights."

"1.20 am. Another distress flare sighted. Have ordered helm to run in on the beat to look closer. Gave firm orders to take heed of the lee shore. Very dangerous."

I leant my back against the wall, watching the surf grinding the sand. The open page lifted in the wind and fell back into place. I knew deep inside that it wasn't a coincidence that I had been given this task. It was for some purpose, something to do with Adam, I felt sure. I re-read the final entry of the log of the *Sea Witch* again. When I finished I had a strange insight, a foreboding - almost as if there stood, back deep behind all the sombre shrouds of the years and the people, a light - not yet glimpsed but waiting to be discovered - and that when I drew back the final curtain to face it, I would have the answer. Then I stopped the thought. My mind had drifted. How could there be an answer? I didn't even have a question.

My foot knocked against more sticks wedged tightly in a pile in the back of the dark corner between the chest and the wall, stained and covered in cobwebs. They looked like kindling wood, but were all of an identical shape. I put the log books on the top of the chest and pulled out one of the sticks. It was about twelve inches long, but half of one end had been cut in the shape of a shallow lipped hammer and was covered in what looked like a thin skin of yellowed bone or ivory.

Adam came and stood beside me. "Do you know what these are, Adam?" I asked him, holding them up, inviting him to speak.

He took one, turning it over in his hands, giving me a sly look. "You already know what they are."

126

He took two white and two black and held them side by side, "If you hold them like this, they look very much like the keys from an old piano, don't they?"

So, I thought, Adam had got his story from the logs of the Sea Witch. But he had embellished the whole thing. Why?

He looked around carefully, came up close. "Read the rest of the story. Nobody can help me."

"I can try."

"Read the rest of the story," He turned, made for the door, turned again, his face angry, "You're all the same, you psychos. String it out, take your time. Get paid." His last words were mixed with the wind as he opened the door wide. "Then fuck off."

18

I needed to get Adam on my side if I was going to make any progress. His anger presented a huge obstacle. He had seen through me. I was in limbo. I needed to get his trust.

I crossed the small pebbled spring-stream at the bridge, just above where it fell over the cliff onto the beach, then followed the narrow lane up to the old church.

Seen close up, the old church was small, no bigger than a small barn, snuggled stockily into the lap of a gentle slope, so old that its creamy yellow stone walls seemed to grow out of the dry grass of the slope itself. A neatly painted sign on the wall discreetly informed the passer-by that it was "The Ancient Church of St. Boniface, Re-built and Dedicated A.D. 1070."

A rusting iron gate opened on to a narrow flint path down to the porch. A group of oblong table-tombs stood by the wall of the church. The graveyard fell away into a steep hollow, the gravestones stacked around its edge in close groups, all at odd angles and in no order, different shapes and sizes - as if thrown together awaiting collection. With difficulty, I squeezed by a large stone plinth reaching a clear space.

I looked at the stone plinth and the figurehead on top of it, secured by an iron bar sunk into the stone in front of a large stone cross. The plinth lay at the very edge of the graveyard, part covered with the shoots and branches of the well-grown hedge next to it. The wooden figurehead was rotten with decay, disfigured by woodworm and weather. One arm had fallen off, jaggedly amputated by rot and where it should have raised in the air in defiant pride, there remained only a pitted and disintegrating stump. A split had begun to run upwards through the body where the iron bar had been inserted at its base and the face was so worn that it was impossible to see features, let alone an expression. The folds of her colourless dress were disfigured with deep mould, the final denigration being given by the thick veneer of bird-droppings covering what seemed to be her crown of thorns, her head and shoulders.

I ran my hand along the dust lying caked in the inscription at the front of the square plinth. 'Sacred to the memory of Captain Edwin Henry Alexander Doe - Master of the ship, "Sea Witch" wrecked off Monks Bay, 23rd Sept. 1849'

My eye caught the shape of other letters engraved on the side of the plinth. Unread and uncleaned for decades, moss and lichen had crept into the grooves of the letters and all I could read were the words, "YE NEED WATCH...."

I brushed and dug at the moss in the crevices of the carved grooves. Uncovering the last letter, I whispered the whole message.

YE NEED WATCH AND PRAY IN FEAR
FOR YE KNOW NOT
WHEN THE CYCLE WILL FULL TURN.

I sat down on a humble stone ledge which had skewed over the years, thick pale green moss at the lower end. The last message of Captain Doe before me, I sat for a long time, feeling lost. As I stood, looking down, I saw the writing under where I had been sitting, my weight having slightly dislodged the moss.

"To the fond memory of Jane Tench, Friend of this Parish, Poor deranged soul who shall forever be remembered. An act of kindness is an antidote to all the evil in this world."

My name. Wise words. I felt the silent reproach of my dead namesake, whoever she had been. I felt humbled. I looked behind me at the darkening trees. All I could hear was a murmur and kiss of the sea and the shore.

PART SEVEN

19

East Dene Manor, Bonchurch, Isle of Wight.
Summer, 1849.

James Wiskard had been drawn into conversation and had wandered away. Rosie came back from her reverie of Joe and suddenly noticed the same maid in the shade of one of the doorways, pointing her out to another skivvy, both shaking their heads. She saw them coming, weaving around the edge of the crowd, the maid intent on revenge. Rosie just stood where she was, watching them coming. The maid rushed up and roughly grabbed her by the arm and pointed through a gate in the hedge. "The other village folk are through there," She said in a loud voice, pushing firmly at Rosie's back. "You, Miss Highty-tighty, 'ee shouldn't be here with the gentry at all!"

Rosie dropped the cup and saucer. It was just bad luck that it broke on the ground - too many sunny days had hardened the earth under the lawn. The maid started yelling, making the most of it, her spiteful vengeance adding to Rosie's helpless embarrassment. Everyone turned to look, the men moving forward, all startled at the noise. The maid was still screeching away. Everyone was looking at her, the whining repetitive screech, "I tole her, she broke it! She broke it! What a proper fist! What will the mistress say? I tole her she shouldn'a ben 'ere, shouldn'a ben 'ere in the first instance, I tole her, the little Fizgig..." The maid gabbled away, eyes wild, finger stabbing. Rosie looked round frantically for Wiskard who had, of course, made himself scarce. She was on her own....

The colour seemed to drain out of everything. The men and women around her seemed impervious to the embarrassment happening right in front of them, whilst at the same time sending out waves of disapproval and managing to look somewhere else. She was petrified, looking around for a kind face in the crowd. Then a face appeared, a young face. Not kind really, but taking command.

"You're a cheap little dollymop. Get your hands off her."

He was young, Nathan. And he was old. But he could certainly stop a crowd when he wanted to. It must have been his days with the barrow-boys in the sludge and turmoil of the London streets. His strident cockney shout had stopped the maid in full flight. Everyone went quiet. It wasn't just his slang (which nobody could have understood), but he had a tremendous, well, presence, you just couldn't ignore him when he chose to make himself felt. He had contrived to place himself right in the middle of the crowd, assuming authority as if their spokesman. They all looked at him standing there, resplendent in his black suit and dandy yellow cravate, his "kingsman" he called it, spilling out sumptuously from an impeccable shirt.

Nathan's voice changed like a ventriloquist, now the lazy drawl of the rest of them, "You're lying. I was watching you. You attacked her." He turned to the rest of the crowd, "Please, Ladies and Gentlemen," He waved them towards the house, "Some more refreshment - I believe that at this moment preparations on the Calotype are being completed... Some of you may wish to volunteer...."

The group laughed as they began to disperse and to float back across the lawn, the scene over. Nathan came up to Rosie and the maid, stooping to pick up the broken cup, laughing under his breath, the harsh cockney coming into his voice again, "Well, well, a ream little muck-snipe nemmo if I ever saw one...." He said to the maid, "Why did you do that? Taking the prejudiced values of your employer against one of your own class? You should know better than that!"

"And you should know better, Nathan Capper, after all I have given you, than to make such an exhibition of yourself!"

Rosie turned at the reproach, spoken quietly from behind her shoulder. A thin tall man with peppery hair and beard stood looking sadly down at Nathan with a moist, rheumy look, a face softened by sentiment and privilege. "Why must you reward me in this lamentable fashion, Nathan? Have you no gratitude?"

Nathan looked up at the man sharply, resentfully. Rosie had time to look carefully at Nathan. She saw a tension between them, a fondness and resentment on both sides, confrontation just beneath the surface, anxiety holding it down.

Nathan's face was perfectly proportioned, almost too perfect, thick, dark waving hair framing a broad brow above dark eyebrows and a long straight nose. Rosie recalled pictures of Greek gods in her school books. Really a classical face, almost waxen in its uncreased perfection. But then the perfectness collapsed as Nathan started pulling hard at his ear lobe, the classical full lips thinned and tightened. He relented and bowed. "Lord Ashburnham, I apologise sir!" He looked as if he meant it.

Lord Ashburnham looked at Nathan with a tender resignation. "Well, then. But please try to remember all that I have taught you." His watery eyes absently gazed past them both, his thin voice taking on the distinct enunciation of a professor examining a theorem, "Consider the situation. Is it not the truth that by castigating this maid, you are as guilty of exercising your new found status as she is of attempting to reflect what she believes are the demands of it?" His pale watery eyes crinkled with kindly good humour. "I see that you still have much to learn." He said, stroking his finger along the pointed beak of his nose, "Not least, in these delicate and sensitive times, to be careful when proclaiming new social theories to those whose ears are not suitably attuned!" He glanced at the maid and waved her away. She curtseyed and fled.

"Nathan, am I not properly surprised that you dare even to attempt to voice such issues on such an occasion as this? To one of Lady Swinburne's menial servants?"

Nathan looked shamefaced. His earlobe reddened as he tugged harder at it.

"Now, will you please be good enough to introduce me?"

"Er, Lord Ashburnham, may I present..."

They both looked enquiringly at Rosie.

"Rose Cotton." She said. She felt small and silly.

"Well, Miss Cotton, I trust that you are enjoying this wonderful day," Ashburnham gazed around him, diplomatically neutralising the atmosphere, "...and these delightful gardens. Certainly, Nathan, I am grateful to you for suggesting that we come here, and for making all the arrangements. A wonderful place. And such delightful company! Delightful." He turned to Rosie, "Mr. Capper here persuaded me to visit Bonchurch and I was extremely reluctant to do so, I may readily confess, because of the extremely onerous demands upon my time," He sniffled and gazed skywards, the light emphasising the ghostly paleness of his eyes.

She smiled and Lord Ashburnham smiled back. His smile was just a trifle watery.

"Yes, and the climate here is indeed unique! I believe that some plants have indeed been found only to grow here in the undercliff beneath the downs." Lord Ashburnham pointed vaguely in the direction of a tree thick with fan-shaped leaves. "That is a Ginko, a tree from Northern China, which Lady Swinburne tells me will not grow even in the new Botanical Gardens at Kew!" He stood looking at the tree, musing, and then, seeming to have forgotten about both of them completely, ambled slowly off towards the french windows.

Nathan turned to Rosie. "You'd better get on...I'll come and find you when it's deadlurk."

Nathan turned and walked away before she could thank him. But of course, he knew the effect he'd had. He always did. There was never anyone so alert to people, so able to manipulate - especially in a crowd. He had chosen to use his costermonger street-slang for a purpose, but you couldn't guess what it was. Maybe he was just experimenting. After all, that was why he was there. He was an experiment. He said it to Rosie at the very end, "I am a social experiment. Nothing more, nothing less." But his secret was that he didn't care. He had suffered so much. It was not caring that gave him his freedom.

Rosie ran through the gate to the other garden. She spotted her father's stocky frame and his face tanned to dark oak beneath white hair and grimy flat-cap. He was with some other fisherman and a travelling tinker who had somehow got through the gates, drinking ale at a trestle table. The women were sitting at another and their children were romping around the lawns in a noisy mêlée. The older boys and girls, of whom Rosie knew several, sat under the branches of a tree also drinking ale, the boys to the south in the sun, the girls separately in the shade, pretending to ignore the boys.

Rosie tapped at her father's shoulder and could see as he turned that he had already had too much beer. A thin white clay pipe lay on the table by his elbow, half-filled with the black tobacco that he regularly brought across the shoreline. He was at the end of telling a loud joke to the raucous group, who slopped ale across the trestle as they laughed and belched. Rosie pressed her lips hard up against his ear as she urgently whispered news of the coastguards' visit. Instantly his good humour had gone. Looking at his eyes, she could see beneath the ale's gloss the yellow residue of cunning. Knowing the signs well, she watched his mouth disappear within the bristly white beard. He was thinking.

The gate from the other garden opened and in came the Rector and Miss Cowan, the mistress of the school, both waddling in their earnest determination to outdo each other in being seen to dispense goodwill amongst the lower classes on this special day. Rosie saw the tension between them. They were annoyed with each other, and had, as happens frequently under the strain to keep up appearances, been unable to finish their argument in time for the ceremonies to begin.

" I still cannot understand why you insist upon introducing these dissenting volumes, or why you cannot accede to the request of the School Committee. You will stand alone, indeed you do stand alone, against the general inclination, by reason of your decided, and may I say vexed, antagonism to Church principles!" Miss Cowan hissed, for all to hear, carried by what had obviously been a heated debate.

"I've told you before, I'll tell you again", spluttered the Rector, "I'll resist the insinuation of the Oxford Movement into this parish. I'll have nothing whatever to do with it! It, or any other High Anglican cant!"

Miss Cowan ran stiffly forward, gaining precedence over the Rector, "All the children first! All the children come with me please! We have a camera obscura by the kitchens. Mothers, please bring the small children."

The women rose quickly and the men rose unsteadily as a belated sign of respect. Children were gathered, the older boys and girls were enticed from under the tree and Rosie followed as they were marched out into a smaller garden carved into a half-circle in the sharp rise of the downs facing the sun. Right in the middle, there was a wood and brass tripod structure with a black curtain draped over it.

A number of gentry boys and girls self-consciously emerged from a drawing-room and stood about waiting with barely-disguised impatience, whilst the Rector and the schoolmistress deferentially fussed about, arranging them in rows sitting at the top of the short slope.

"Rosie Cotton!" Her name called last, Rosie walked forward as daintily as she could, aware of the furtive eyes of the older boys and the appraisal of the girls, as they sat in stiff anticipation. As she took her place, she was glad that she wasn't so tall that more than the top half of her smock could be seen above the heads of the boys and girls in front below her. Turning to glance above, she saw the rich boys with straw boater hats and beautifully-tailored short coats and knee-breeches, some with bow ties and even watch-chains, and the rich girls in velvet and lace. The middle row was taken by the sons and daughters of the new tradesmen and the builders - good quality clothes, but more plain. And then, finally, the bottom two rows where Rosie sat with the children she had grown up with along the shore and in the tiny village, before the rich and their tradesmen had come. Looking at their bare feet, she was glad that she had managed to find the old boots, however painful, but hoped that the photographer would not show them in the photograph.

Captain and Lady Jane Swinburne entered with their children, Algernon, Edith and Alice, followed by a small man with long, dark waving hair, falling in a mop over one eyebrow and brushed back forcefully across the top and over the other side of his head, curling over his ears in "jug-loops". He wore a pair of unusually loud checked trousers, a low-slung double-breasted waistcoat with large lapels and a high-necked shirt with a large and fulsome cravate, secured with a gold pin. He stood looking about him, clearly waiting to be introduced. He looked exhausted.

Miss Cowan took the cue. "Children," she called prettily, "Children! I am deeply honoured, and very proud," She glanced at the man, smiling, enlisting his understanding.

The man gave it. "Children!" He bellowed, "I am Charles Dickens, the very famous author! The Inimitable! And," He glanced slyly at Miss Cowan before making a low sweeping bow, "I am very pleased to make your acquaintance, being here to officiate at your prize-giving ceremony."

Miss Cowan giggled and, given the signal, everyone smiled. "I am sure that all of you know of Mister Dickens' works and will not need to be reminded that he is currently staying across the lane at Winterbourne, where he is engaged upon writing the Personal History of David Copperfield."

All clapped. Seats were brought in and the notables sat, whilst the younger children stood up in a line and recited a poem about a clock (may we always be like the clock, which is always doing its duty by others and always tells the truth, etcetera) and then recited their multiplication tables. Charles Dickens had raised his face to the sun and had closed his eyes, as if in peaceful concentration.

Then at last came the prize-giving. Charles Dickens stood and handed the prizes from a table as Miss Cowan read out the names of the winners and the subjects for which they had won, accompanied by a sprinkling of applause. After about half an hour, as the rather tired applause for the last winner had died down, Miss Cowan paused and looked up at the ranks of seated children. "Lastly, I come to the prize for the best and most rapid progress during the Term. And I would like to say, before naming the recipient of this prize, that despite her station in life the winner has excelled against all conceivable odds to achieve a remarkable progress. Particularly in written composition and grammar. Her written fiction is quite remarkable and her poems are a source of joy to us all. We will all be very sorry to see her leave our little school as she now prepares to step out into the world. We will miss you. Our heartfelt congratulations to Miss Rose Olivia Cotton. Rosie Cotton!" Everyone clapped with the renewed energy given by realising that this was the last prize.

Rosie stepped down with humility, hoping to see her father in the crowd. But he was nowhere to be seen. She approached Mister Dickens, who took a small leather-bound volume from Miss Cowan and presented it to Rosie. His eyes held a strange expression as he looked at her. "And what is your station in life?" He asked gently, handing her the book. It was unfair of him to ask it, then,

Rosie thought, in front of all these people. But his tone made her sure that it was not meant maliciously, and she answered him directly.

"My father is a fisherman, sir. My mother is dead" And then, as an afterthought, "I live on the beach."

A sudden humorous warmth shone in his eyes, transforming his expression, "In a house, I hope, not in an upturned boat!" The tiredness had left him, and he looked at her closely, carefully.

"In a cottage, sir, down there on the beach." Rosie gestured with the hand holding the book, "We have enough to live on."

"Then you are indeed fortunate in these difficult times." He spoke as if ending the conversation, but changed his mind, "We plan to play some rounders on that beach, and have picnics." He said, gaily, "and a man is building me a shower-house under the waterfall at this very minute. Since you are now so adept at written composition and grammar, you could help me by reading my drafts... as my young sister-in-law did before she died." Dickens paused. "You remind me of her." These last words had slipped out, as if without intention, and his tone touched Rosie with its sadness.

She paused, "I would like it very much, sir."

The Rector coughed and the schoolmistress touched Rosie's elbow. Rosie was suddenly conscious that everyone was waiting for her to stop talking. Dickens ignored them, holding up his hand. "Tell me about your stories."

Rosie couldn't fight her awareness of everyone fidgeting, their impatience to get on, blurting out, "I don't know how it is," She said quickly, her mind on the Rector and Miss Cowan, "My head can never pick and choose its people." She shrugged, now anxious to finish the conversation, "They come and they go, and they don't come and they don't go, just as they like." She shook hands with the great man and returned to her seat, conscious of everyone's eyes upon her. She glanced down at the volume which she had won it. It was a leather-bound copy of Elizabeth M. Sewell's "Readings For Every Day In Lent". She glanced up at the clear sky. "Thank you, Mama." she whispered.

From inside the huge black curtain on top of the wooden tripod, the photographer shouted muffled instructions to keep perfectly still "until further notice". Just at the last moment, Rosie felt her side shoved as a dark figure dropped into place beside her. It was Nathan Capper. She was surprised by his strong smell of cologne, now that he was so close, as if he had only just applied it to his smooth cheeks from a scent-bottle in over-enthusiastic amounts. He had combed his hair too, she noticed. Her nostrils thick with his scent, Rosie managed to slide a question out of the corner of her mouth, "Where are you from?"

She heard his laugh before his answer, "From the Holy Land". Rosie stared back at the camera as they had all been told. There followed what seemed long minutes of waiting in the sunlight, all trying not to blink or move their heads. Rosie was not only thinking about Nathan. She was thinking about other things. About Charles Dickens, about her hurt and disappointment at her father's absence from the prize-giving, about the photograph, about time. Frozen in time, Rosie thought, frozen for ever. In a hundred years, people might see a faded copy of this Calotype photograph and wonder who we were, not noticing the differences in our dress, not realising that the ones at the bottom were so totally separate from all the rows above them. And that I am separate from them all.

The photographer stood up and shouted that the photograph had been taken, then pulled something out of the camera and rushed into the tent behind him. Rosie got to her feet and cursed. Too late, she saw the Rector standing beside her, sharply disapproving. Catching his eye, she quickly looked down again at the big dark smear which covered the top of her white sleeve where she had wiped her mouth with it. The rusty stain was bound to show up clearly in the photograph. She hadn't noticed it before - everyone must have seen it. She shrugged defiantly. Nobody was ever likely to give her a copy of the picture, anyway. Forcing herself to smile at the Rector, Rosie turned away from Nathan and the rest of them to search for her father. She strolled back to the other garden, only to find it completely empty, the trestle tables deserted, littered with mugs and earthenware jars. Turning to leave, she stopped at a sound. A small gate in the sandstone wall, which she hadn't noticed before, had opened and then her father emerged, deep in discussion with James Wiskard. They both looked very serious. Wiskard, red-faced, waved an envelope under her father's nose. Her father was glum and thoughtful, his mouth out of sight beneath his beard. The envelope was strange. It was printed in bright blue with a picture of figures on it.

Both men were so absorbed that neither noticed her standing there until they were close. When they caught sight of her, Rosie thought she saw a definite and formidable expression in both of Wiskard's eyes, that both were staring at her directly. Looking at her father, she saw the same angry alarm in his expression. Wiskard quickly put the bright blue envelope in an inner pocket of his coat and her father took a step forward, making to blurt something at her, but Wiskard's grip on his arm drew him back, "Say nothing to her! Nothing!" She heard the hoarse whisper distinctly. They stood looking at her, both controlling their expressions, silent. Quickly calculating, Rosie realised that the two men must have been talking together on the other side of the wall for at least an hour.

20

There was a small sound behind her. By the sudden sharp smell of cologne, Rosie knew before she swivelled round that it was Nathan Capper whose boot had just scraped on the flagstones. She caught him lowering his arm, as if he had just made a signal to the two men by the gate. All three stood unnaturally still, each visibly trying to disown the guilty intrigue which her intuition saw thick in the air between them. The only times Rosie had seen her father like this was when he was planning a smuggling run. Her only surprise was just how guilty they looked.

Well, Rosie thought, she had warned him of the gobbies, after all. If he wanted to take the risk of another run, that was up to him. She decided to pretend not to notice and turned and walked quickly through the garden past the departing guests. Still, she admitted that she had felt a shock. She was astonished that the two grown men had looked so terrified at having been discovered together, looking so much like conspirators.

But she put her suspicions out of her mind as Nathan caught up with her. "I'll walk with you." He offered. And then, lamely, "I have never walked on a beach before."

She nodded her assent, nervous and pleased, and together they silently began the stroll out through the gates, passing round the rump of the turrets opposite Winterbourne and down the steep lane beside the old church. Unbearably self-conscious with the struggle to find something to say, Rosie stopped by the stone wall and ran her hand across the smooth moss and round sandstone on its flanks, glad of its reassuring feel.

She looked over the wall and remembered her mother lying over the other side with the body of her small baby, her sister. She suddenly lifted the book she was carrying, planted a kiss on its cover and blew the kiss over the wall.

"What are you doing?"

She looked up at Nathan. She had forgotten that he was there, "Nothing, just paying my respects." She changed subject, "You know they built a new church? Just above East Dene?"

"Yes," answered Nathan, "I saw it when Lord Ashburnham and I arrived on that bone-shaking coach." He smiled at her. "We went through more than thirty fields to get here from the ferry at Ryde pier. I counted them to pass the time. The gate boy spent a full three minutes at each gate, opening, closing each one....it took three hours and thirty-eight minutes. I timed it." Nathan slipped a silver watch on a chain from his waistcoat, prised open the lid with his thumb and looked at it. "More time than the London and South-Western Railway from London to Southampton. How far is it to Ryde?"

He was so worldly, Rosie thought. How could she say that she had never been to Ryde? "Not far."

"No more than twelve miles, I would say." He rested his back against the wall and began, too, to smooth the warm stones on the top of it. "We should have brought Ashburnham's carriage, but then the Mary

Blaine's" - he stopped and corrected himself, "I mean, the train's, much faster and at one pound for a four-wheeler on the ferry and five shillings for each horse! Extortion. And they still tow the carriages in a barge behind the steamer! And we would have to wait for the tide to get it onto dry land! And the fare cost us a duce hog between us! Two shillings!"

Those funny words. They made her nervous. He seemed foreign, almost talking to himself in his own private language, not realising she couldn't have understood. Never having ridden in a carriage, unable to share the knowledge and complaints of this sophisticated traveller, Rosie decided it was better to get back onto her own safe ground. "This is very old, you know. The church of St. Boniface, nearly a thousand years old."

She remembered what he had told her in front of the camera, "Why did you say you were from the Holy Land?"

Nathan's face fell. The sophisticated young man disappeared. Such dark eyes, she thought, seeing pain crease his face, now much younger - almost a boy, incongruous in his smart, flamboyant clothes.

"Because that is what it is called." He said slowly.

He started to walk along beside the wall, keeping his fingers running along the top. Rosie followed him to the gate. He went into the graveyard and sat on a flat tombstone. She sat beside him, giving him time, fascinated. "What is it?" She asked softly, after a lull.

He straightened up. His voice was low when he spoke, but had reverted to the strange brashness she had heard on the lawn, challenging her.

"From my square rig and smart crabshells, you wouldn't think I was coopered, would you?"

She wasn't going to be put down. She was getting impatient with this game. "You think it clever to talk like that? Why can't you just answer the question? What is the Holy Land?"

He relented, the confident young man again. "Yes. I'm puckering. It's the language we speak," Again he stopped, *"They* speak in the Holy Land. It's the language of the criminal underworld. The swell mob, the maltoolers." Nathan looked around at the quiet churchyard, sun-dappled by the trees, "A million miles from here..." He suddenly shrugged and his face stiffened, "...and I've never really lost it. I'll never forget."

"Have you read Oliver Twist?" Nathan continued, "No? Well, now you're so good at reading, why don't you ask that fabulist Dickens to lend you a copy? Or, even better, ask him. He knows the district very well indeed. He's had a conducted tour with police at midnight, with no less than Officer Restiaux himself, I believe, or maybe it was Inspector Field. One of them, anyway. One of the few peelers who knew how to get in and out. I saw Dickens, but he wouldn't remember my face, thank God. I was one of three hundred he must have seen that night. The Holy Land is eight acres where God does not exist. A nest of thieves, a stinking cholera-riven compost heap for the surplus population, hopeless people, the outcasts in the back settlements and the netherskens. The *dangerous classes.* I slept and lived in a room with twenty people in it." He winced, laughing shortly. "Whole families, mothers with children and babies, starving and desperate. The

148

stink was appalling. Everyone used to piss outside the front door and shit in the alley. Men and women the same. And more than that at night, more crowded than those graves." He pointed to a cluster of tombs, shouldered unevenly together in the far corner under a tree. "They were at it even in the afternoon, when there was more space, the dollies and their men, tails in the air, often six or more pairs in a room, hard at it on the filthy straw, like animals. And so was everyone else, naked in the heat and stench, like maggots in a cheese."

Rosie tried to keep the shock off her face. She looked at the far tombs, trying not to imagine such horror. But Nathan wouldn't stop. She had asked a question and now she was getting the answer in full. Nathan's voice began to shake at his memories. "The disease was terrible. Living there, trying to keep alive. It was worse than anything Dickens said in Oliver Twist, bless him. There was a lake in the yard which was a cesspool, stagnant, thick with dead dogs and cats, putrefying, bubbling. Sometimes there were dead babies."

He suddenly switched mood again and laughed. "It's New Oxford Street now."

"But anyone looking at you and listening to you would be fooled!" She protested.

"Yes. Ashburnham's work. He's done a good job on me." He stood up and walked along the path to the porch, taking in the gravestones, speaking to her over his shoulder, "Elocution lessons." Still bent over, arm in the air, he looked back at her down the row of gravestones, struck by a sudden thought. "My father would have been proud." He said bitterly, with a clutch in his throat. He stopped. He had said enough, too much. After a pause, the thought cleared. "What are you doing tomorrow, Rosie?"

Holding back a stream of questions, Rosie knew the conversation was ending, "I will go higgling in Ventnor. Selling crabs."

"Shall I be permitted to accompany you? I could show you some coster tricks I picked up. You might sell more, honest."

Rosie laughed, charmed by this handsome young man who could so easily switch from mood to mood, from accent to accent, voice to voice. Charmed and intrigued by his boyish enthusiasm about a chore. Intrigued by his past and his nervy unsettledness. Sympathising with his sadness for his father, sharing it with her feelings for her own mother, so easily remembered. Wanting to know more about him, the darkness she had seen in there. She felt sorry for him. It would be nice to have him with her, she decided.

"Yes, you may. But I have to leave early. An hour after sunrise. About half past six o'clock, I believe. I collect the crabs and lobster from the fisherman on the beach - along the cove by the waterfall. Down there." She pointed to where the stream along the side of the graveyard disappeared over the cliff.

"Well enough. I'll meet you then. Goodbye, Rosie." Without another word, Nathan Capper stood up straight, walked past Rosie and out of the church gate.

Although she stayed waiting for him to turn and wave to her from the corner, he didn't look back, carrying his nightmares with him. Rosie was disappointed.

150

21

Rosie scrubbed the last of the tin plates in the bucket of sea-water and then searched behind the piles of nets for two big earthenware jugs. She had heard that they were piping fresh water into the new houses on the downs, available at the mere turn of a tap - the height of luxury she thought, remembering her endless thrice-daily journeys with a bucket along the sand to the spring which fell, by the side of the old church, in the waterfall at Horseshoe Bay. Since her mother had died, Rosie had done most of the housework in the cottage. Since Joe had gone away to sea, she had done it all. She had soon learned that if she didn't change the straw and wash the bedding and clean the pots, they stayed dirty. She thought again about the first Bargain Saturday in Newport, now soon, the 20th September. Would she find work? Would a farmer take her on? She shrugged and leant to pick up the jugs. Any work on a farm would just be more of the same drudgery. But she hoped that she would find someone kind. That's all she asked, really, she thought. That's what it came down to in the end, all said and done.

A whole month had gone since the coastguards had come and there had been no further runs of brandy across the shoreline. Worse, the tubs hidden in the cliff still lay there, the risk of moving them too great. Money was short. Her father had been drunk all the time on grog - a costly mix of spirit and ale and no longer even made a pretence of being a fisherman. Desperate, Rosie had started higgling. What with this, the cooking and the housework, she felt exhausted. But now, because of his drinking, she soon wouldn't even afford the three shillings needed to buy the crabs, lobsters and prawns she needed to "higgle" - to buy them fresh from the real fishermen and to hawk them round the town in a basket, which had up till now given them a profit of two shillings a day.

Rosie thought of Joe every day as she worked. She was certain that he was on his way home. The feeling in her had got stronger and stronger, sometimes so strong she found that she had stopped what she was doing and caught herself gazing blankly at the floor, mop or brush or knife in hand. When she let herself, she could actually feel him getting closer by the day, her mind reaching out over the ocean like a light to guide him home. She constantly told herself that it was her imagination, that it couldn't be real, that she shouldn't be so stupid and that it was only wishful thinking. But still she felt it. Stronger and stronger every day. She longed to see his flashing smile and bright laughter and to feel his clean strength, her darling brother. But her feelings ran up against her common sense telling her to be sensible, that it was only sensible that she must give up hope that he would ever return. Nevertheless, every night, whilst her father snored on the wooden platform above her head, she stared into the rafters and lifted a prayer that Joe was still alive and would come back. Come back before she went away.

Now, every night, as she thought of the loneliness of her life, she didn't even try to hold back the tears as she said her prayers. Her father was rarely home or was too drunk to hear. Every night, Rosie desperately hoped that there was really someone listening, hoped that her fervent prayers would be heard by someone, someone beyond the lonely black arch of the rafters and the thatched roof. Somebody kind. Somebody who wouldn't care about her father, the smuggling, the drinking. Someone who would bring Joe back to get her and take her away. If he came home before Bargain Saturday, she thought, the two of them would be able to offer themselves for work together.

She put the jugs in the shaped wicker basket, picked up the bucket, and set off across the stones. She drew round the headland and went to the waterfall, used now to the extra tiresome task of having to climb up the cliff a bit in order to fill the jugs from the falling water before it disappeared and splashed into the old punctured bath perched on the top of the hut, which the men had built so that Mister Dickens could take his shower privately in the water spraying through the holes in the bottom of the bath.

But this time, she saw soap lather sliding with the rush of water emerging from under the closed door and from within heard the sound of a sing-song voice, shouting out, *"Rhia Rhama Rhoos, the Unparalleled...."* The voice paused, there was the thin sound of a scrubbing brush, then the voice recommenced with more certainty, "Rhia Rhama Rhoos, the Unparalleled Necromancer!"

Rosie stood, undecided to go ahead and collect the water or to return to her cottage and come back later.

The voice continued with the largesse of a fairground crier, warbling in the force of the showering water, "...Presents The Conflagration Wonder.... A card

154

being drawn from the pack by any lady... by any lady not under a direct and positive promise of marriage will....will be immediately named by The Necromancer, then destroyed by fire .... and then reproduced from its own ashes! *Hurrahhhh..."*

Since the voice seemed so absorbed in itself and enjoying itself so much, Rosie decided she could risk quietly sneaking up the slope to get the water. But as Rosie got to the small ledge, she noticed with great embarrassment that she could see, through the gap between the high rim of the hut's wall and the bottom of the old bathtub, in the midst of the water gushing and spraying from the holes in its underside, Mister Dickens wearing a comical black pointed cap, naked in the falling water. Worse, in the middle of declaiming about "The Great Pudding Wonder", he suddenly raised both arms skyward and looked up with another "Hurrah!"

Their eyes met.

Rosie looked away, quickly. She filled both jugs, replaced them in the carrying basket, and leapt down to the safety of the sand.

The door of the hut opened and Mister Dickens stood there, wearing a hastily-put-on and damp pair of trousers. He had taken off the hat.

"I have a confession to make." He said rapidly, earnestly. He spoke with a slight lisp, which she hadn't noticed at the prize-giving. Suddenly seeing how funny he looked, all ideas of the high-minded respect shown by the Miss Cowan for the great author slipped away like the soap suds being washed from his feet by the water. Rosie put down the basket and laughed aloud, rocking on her

155

feet, pointing at him, shaking her head as waves of laughter filled her and erupted. It was the first laughter for a very long time.

Dickens smiled and gestured his helplessness, standing in mock reproach until she had finished shaking with laughter.

"I was rehearsing," He said, mockingly grandiose, "for my great performance of the art of legerdemain, the great and secret art of magic. And," He finished, decidedly, "I would be grateful if you would please accept my invitation to attend... As I said," He smiled, wiping a speck of soap from his eyes, "I have a confession."

"What is it that you wish to confess, pray Mister Dickens?" Entering into the spirit of the game, Rosie felt drawn to him, to his readiness to laugh at himself, his humour so near the surface.

"Theft!" He cried, sinking to his knees, "I have stolen something of yours."

Rosie looked around him, looked back at him, perplexed.

"I am a plagiarist. For the first time have I stolen words wholesale from another author. Authoress." He corrected himself, "Please tell nobody of this dreadful secret. In return you can come to my magic party instead of getting a copyright royalty, and thus avoid the distress of further piratic copying of your, *our* property by our American cousins, a problem very dear to my heart, I may say."

"But what words have you stolen from me?" Rosie couldn't think of anything she had written or said that anyone had thought worth listening to, let alone repeating.

Dickens, now dry, reached into the hut for his shirt. Buttoning it up, searching in his memory, he suddenly raised his voice into a soft maidenly giggle, "Lor, Peggotty!" observed my mother, rousing herself from a reverie, "what nonsense you do talk!" His voice changed to a matronly warmth, touched by toil and good-nature, "Well, but I really do wonder, ma'am," said Peggotty..." Back came the tittering voice of the empty-headed girl, "What can have put such a person in your head?" inquired my mother. "Is there nobody else in the world to come there?" Mister Dickens paused, winked at Rosie, and then said slowly in the soft whimsical Sussex burr of the matron, emphasising every word, *"I don't know how it is," said Peggotty, "unless it's on account of being stupid, but my head can never pick and choose its people, they come and they go, and they don't come and they go, just as they like.................................* "

"There," he said, "Chapter Seven of David Copperfield. Your words. You said them to me when I gave you your prize. That very worthy book." He reached for his boots and jacket. "They are in the Third Issue of Copperfield, already published. Come to the pond at nine. We're all going for a picnic on the Down and then I shall give my inimitable magic performance!" He brought a comb from his jacket pocket and began combing his damp hair across the top of his head.

"Well, thank you Mr. Dickens. But I don't know if I can. I have to sell crabs today."

"Nonsense. Let the crabs wait for one day in their pots. Grant them one more day of salty saline happiness!

157

Promise me you'll come. Afterwords, I'll read you the result of my latest efforts, Chapter Thirteen. Remember, Miss Rosie Cotton, we authors have to be punctual! To meet deadlines is the only way to meet the endless tribe of bills from our creditors! At the pond at nine o'clock?"

He was mad, thought Rosie. But he was fun. It was time she had some fun. "Yes, I'll come," She said. She would have to wear the lace smock again or the dress Joe had bought her before he left. She mentally abandoned her plan to go higgling, but then remembered that Nathan was going to meet her on the beach. She would have to explain the new plan to Nathan.

Dismissed by Dickens who had started up the path in the opposite direction, Rosie picked up her jugs. Then she stopped and shouted up at Dicken's departing back. "There's just one thing, Mr. Dickens!"

"And what is that, Miss Cotton?" He said, turning from his climb and looking down at her.

"I don't recall saying that I was stupid!"

"Well then, my dear, you have just proved your point! Indeed you didn't say that. But you will allow the great author to add a few artistic embellishments. You have a good memory, essential for the craft. I look forward to reading your first book!"

With a quick wave, he reached the top of the low cliff and disappeared. Rosie ambled back to the cottage along the hem of the bubbling surf, thinking. Thinking about an inconceivable idea, just glimpsed. She struggled with the bigness of it and her inclination to dismiss it as moonshine. But then she shrugged, she would never know if she didn't try. When she next took the crabs to

Ventnor, she would spend some of her little money on ink and paper and a quill and pen-knife, or maybe a new pen with a steel nib.

As she put the jugs down in a cool corner of the cottage, she heard a soft rap on the frame of the open door. Outside stood Nathan. He was dressed in more ordinary clothes than he had worn at the prize-giving, plain woollen breaches, a light jacket and a blue double-breasted waistcoat with pearl buttons, but still with a kingsman scarf, this time of green silk with blue dots. He seemed out of breath. Quickly, she put her finger to her lips. Her father was still asleep. She ran through the door and pulled it gently behind her.

Nathan was agitated, shifting from one foot to the other, one hand behind his back. "I was scared that I would miss you. I am sorry, but I cannot come with you today," He pulled off his flat hat, "The Dickens party are going for a picnic on the top of Boniface Down and Ashburnham and I have been invited. We have to go. I'm sorry. But I brought you this." He took his hand from behind his back to show a paper parcel, wrapped with red silk ribbon.

She took the heavy package from him and moved off to the side along the pebbles, drawing him with her, looking back nervously at the cottage. Rosie thought suddenly how strange it was that she had received two presents in three days from people she had only just met. First the Frenchman on the shore and now Nathan. Only Joseph had given her presents up till now. Now everyone had begun to do it. "Thank you Nathan, thank you very much. But please could I ask you to speak a little more quietly? My father is in the cottage there, still asleep. If he wakes too early, he has a devil's temper. I wanted to leave before he woke."

Nathan took her arm and moved further along the beach to some large dry rocks. "I know about him, don't worry, soon his troubles will all be over," He whispered impatiently, "Now aren't you going to open it?"

Just too late he straightened his face. She had seen him wince and his face fall back. With a cold feeling she glanced along the sand and up at the cliffs. What did he know? Why would all her father's troubles be over? Was it the gobbies? Knowing that it was the wrong time to ask, she decided that she would have to wait and get it from him later, by deceit if necessary. But she would have to find out quickly. Nathan was watching her carefully. She decided to put the problem firmly in the back of her mind. If he knew something about trouble with the coastguards, she was certain she would be able to get it out of him. She sat on a rock and began to open the parcel. Inside, carefully wrapped in soft tissue paper, was a beautiful set of inkwells in wrought silver and crystal, set in a dark jade-green leather-covered base. They sparkled and shone like jewels in the sun.

"Oh! Nathan, they are so beautiful! I was only just now, just this very moment, thinking of beginning, of trying to write a story!" She looked up at him, "Or even some poems. Nathan, they are lovely!"

"Not as lovely as you are." Nathan blurted, his pale cheeks colouring red. Then he laughed and pulled at his earlobe.

She laughed with him and with joy at the gift. "Now I will have no excuse at all." She stood and kissed him lightly on both cheeks. "I will start writing tomorrow!"

"All you need is something to write about, Rosie."

"Oh! But that's not a problem. After all, as I say, those characters, those stories, they just come and they go, and they don't come and they don't go, just as they like!"

"Well, let's hope they come more than they don't!" He looked out to sea, picked up a pebble and threw it out. In the pause, Rosie anxiously recalled memories of what Nathan had said about the Holy Land. Try as she might, she couldn't get rid of an unease, something wrong, something she was feeling with her intuition, something she couldn't put her finger on. Unintentionally her voice sharpened. "Nathan, these inkstands must have cost a fortune. Where did you get them?"

Nathan smiled grimly, recognising the suspicion in her voice. He looked out at the sea again, squinting in the light and at his memories. "They were my father's. I grabbed them before the bailiffs could take them after he died. They are all that I have left of him and they, well, they sort of kept me alive too." He said. "I have been carrying them for a year now, carrying them in a sack, sleeping with them under my head, since the Kennington Common March of last year when my father was killed by the soldiers." He looked back at her and Rosie saw the tears forming in the edges of his eyes, the anger and loss forming in his chest. "The tenth of April 1848. Whilst the Queen was skulking on this very Island at her huge retreat at Osborne and the fat owners and capitalists sat in parliament, waiting for the great Chartist leader, Feargus

161

O'Connor to be brought to heel, to be cowed. I still sleep with them, these inkstands, even after Ashburnham took me on. Pa used to write his pamphlets with them before they were sent to the printer. He used to write articles for *The Northern Star.* His great Chartist dialogues, his calls for the vote, the franchise, for a free world. I have no better use for them now. He's gone for good. I am not a true writer." He shrugged off the wistfulness. "You can be."

Rose remembered hearing rumours of the Chartists. There had been trouble the previous year in Newport, only fifteen miles away, when the local elections were held. Rumours of smashed windows and discontent. "How did they keep you alive, then, Nathan, I mean the inkstands?"

"My father taught me to write. His only gift, but a great one. He taught me vision, imagination, to see things as they might have been, as they might be. In the Holy Land I used it, but," He smiled again and shrugged, "In a debased manner."

"What did you write, then?"

"I was a screever. I wrote begging letters. For a deaner and a downer a time, two shillings and sixpence a letter, one shining alderman for every letter I wrote. It kept me alive, well alive. And it kept the beggars alive too. I concocted stories and faked official documents, fake testimonials and such like, with gammy monickers. False signatures. I became well known." A note of pride had crept into his voice. He lifted his flat cap and smoothed back his thick dark hair. "At last, I moved into respectable lodgings. I became Respectable. Or half of me did. I worked for a solicitor as a clerk in the day and as a screever at night. Then I was recommended to another solicitor in the Temple. Ashburnham's solicitor. One day, Ashburnham arrived at the solicitor's chambers at lunchtime, unexpected. I was the only one there. He had just come from a debate in the House of Lords and asked me what I thought. He is a liberal, you know, a forward-thinking man with a conscience, a great humanist who is acutely aware of how the government is losing its grip in this modern world. I told him what I thought of the Government's position. Without intending it, I began to tell him of my father's politics, his theories. Then I told him how my father had died. Ashburnham listened. When I finished, he offered me a position as his private secretary. By then, I could supply references."

He grinned at her. "So there you find me, a foot in both camps. I stopped screeving, but of course didn't tell him, Ashburnham, about it. And now I am responsible for all his arrangements. I brought him down here. For his health, you understand, I was worried about his health." He remembered something, "Oh, yes. Before I forget. I brought you the volume I spoke of." He pulled a book out of his pocket, and showed her the cover, *The Undercliff of the Isle of Wight.* "I was reading it last night. Here now, you can tell me if this particular passage is correct. Doctor Martin says here...." He flipped randomly through the pages and then read aloud from the book, stooping, head at an angle, mimicking the slow precise manner and tone of a shortsighted elderly doctor, "....I shall now allude to the inhabitants of the district...." Nathan gave Rosie a pointed look over the top of the book, "Uhmm, Uhmm,...Yes. Ah." He cleared his throat. "The lower orders of the people are generally tall, well-looking and healthy... very little illness of any kind prevails...free from epidemics, Ah yes, here we are! The health and vigour of the labouring classes. It says here, the villagers of Bonchurch especially, are, generally speaking, stalwart and tall *and the women, when young, by no means deficient in personal beauty.....*" Nathan straightened up and went back to his normal voice, laughing, "Well, that was written only last year and published this year." He looked at her slily. "I think Dr. Martin must be writing about you, Miss Cotton!"

Rosie glanced up at him, embarrassed and pleased, "I have never had the pleasure of meeting Doctor Martin!"

"He is obviously no mean authority in his field. Especially on that point."

Nathan looked at her. She looked at him.

Nathan looked away, reddening, tugging at his ear. He looked at the book again. "It says here that the Undercliff is remarkably free from thunder storms, hardly been known it says.... Anyway, here you are." He handed her the book and sat down on the rock. "You can read all about the place you live in, in scientific detail. Climate, temperature, atmospheric pressure, rainfall. You must be flabbergasted at the attention, Rosie. Geology, botany, even hints for invalids.." Suddenly, he paused. His voice softened, went inwards, "...to keep the mind of the sick person from dwelling too much on his own state..."

His tone alarmed her, she saw that he was talking about himself. "Do you? Are you sick?" Rosie was alarmed, "Sickness from the Holy Land?"

He shrugged. He still looked inward. "I am sure that whatever sickness I have will be cured in this place." He said slowly. "Everything will come right in this place." He picked up a flint and knocked it against the blue ovals of some old mussel shells which were hanging from dried seaweed stuck to the rock, crushing them one by one, his face pale, distracted. He beat the flint into the fragile shells, each word followed by the snap and crush of a shell as its delicate resistance was broken. "Everything. Will. Come. Right. In. This. Place. *Everything. Will. Come. Right. In. This. Place.*"

He lost himself in a long pause. Then he came back to her. "But I still have the old contacts in the Holy Land and I still use them sometimes, meeting in secret at night. I suppose you think I'm evil."

"Well, hardly I do." She laughed, deciding to share a few truths. "If screeving kept you alive, it kept you alive." She pointed to her cottage. "In there, at this very moment, snores a smuggler. We, and many others along the shoreline."

Nathan laughed. "Well, at least our crimes aren't that common!" He didn't look at all surprised.

Rosie laughed too. Then she remembered her question. She believed that she could be frank with him now. "Nathan, what did you mean about my father when you said that all of his troubles would be over? Have you heard something about the gobbies? The coastguards?"

Nathan looked at her, startled. "No, I've heard nothing. Nothing at all. I didn't mean anything at all." He stood up suddenly. "I'd better be going to the pond. They'll all be leaving."

"But I'm coming too!" Said Rosie, pleased, "Charles Dickens invited me!"

Nathan's delight and surprise brought the blood back, the waxy pallour leaving his face. "Well, I will see you at the pond in ten minutes." He said and ran up the cliff path.

She turned back to the cottage. Out of the corner of her eye, she saw Nathan turn at the top of the cliff and wave down at her. She looked up, carefully shifted the precious inkstand to one hip, and waved back to him, the heavy book in hand.

22

At nine o'clock, the Dickens party all congregated by the pond, with much fussing about who would ride with whom and checking the food, hampers, linen, tables and cutlery. There were five carts in all, with four adults in each cart. In the back of one there stood a big iron cauldron for boiling potatoes.

By the muddy withy pool in Bonchurch village, the labourers' wives in the string of tiny thatched cottages along Shepherd's Lane and their children had all looked on with quiet amusement, the ragged children running about, the mothers leaning in the low, narrow doorways. In the stonemason's yard in the middle of the cottages a man stood scratching his head before a block of sandstone, like a big lump of cut butter, pale primrose in the sun.

Lord Ashburnham had stayed behind in Ribbands Hotel, pleading weakness of the knees. From the start, it was clear that Charles Dickens had a bad cough and was in a bad mood. When Kate Dickens tried to enlist his help in getting their eight childen in an orderly fashion into the back of one cart, he muttered that his difficult tribe well qualified him to manage a baby farm and that he would give up writing - at least then he would be able to pay all his bills. Everyone tried to ignore the bad feeling, sympathising with Kate who looked tired, dulled and long-suffering and who was having a difficult time with her latest child, a boy of one-and-a-half.

The Rector's wife took exception to Dickens' remark, and noisily reminded him of his article in the Examiner the year before about a baby farm which he had sarcastically called the "Paradise of Tooting", where the owner Drouet had discovered cholera amongst the fourteen hundred abandoned and starving babies and young children in his care, and the parish churchyard had been found too small to hold the piles of tiny coffins.

Dickens looked upset, sulky and rather ill. He announced that he had decided that he would not, after all, perform the great display of magic. It would have to wait till he felt better. He deliberately declined to travel with his wife and children and gave them only a curt wave as their cart trundled along the mud at the side of the pond, past the willows and disappeared up the slope towards Ventnor.

Nathan also stayed behind and made himself politely helpful and concerned with the preparations as each cart was filled and sent off. When the last cart was ready, he still hung back. Rosie was late. Dickens and John Leech, the artist, sat in the back of the cart, talking listlessly, "....that climb is nearly eight hundred feet straight up the side of St. Boniface Down. It's really too much, particularly today." Dickens' voice droned as he stretched his legs out and curled his arms over the side of the cart, trying to get more comfortable,

"I usually think that vigorous exercise gets rid of listlessness, but not today" He coughed raucously, "Not with this confounded cough..."

Nathan hopped from one foot to another at the edge of the pond, disguising his anxiety, and attempted to ignore the village families who examined him with indolent curiosity from the doorways and the small gardens, when they thought he wasn't looking. It began to get hotter. He hated waiting. In the shimmering air he listened to the rise and fall of Dickens' voice.

"....My legs tremble under me all the time, my arms quiver... Look!" Dickens held them up, shaking, to show Leech, "I have incessant dreams, unutterably depressing, I feel I want to cry." Another cough. "...I can't read, I can't write, I feel I have a ball of boiling fat behind my nose and between my eyes."

Then Rosie came running down the narrow lane between the cottages from the direction of East Dene. She wore her best dress which Joe had bought her, the dark green velvet shining in the sunlight, her hair flying as she ran. She looked beautiful.

Nathan stood watching her running towards him, and so did the few wives who still stood in the doorways who looked on with amused complicity, nudging each other, calling inside for their daughters to come and look. "Here you!" One of them called out loudly enough for Nathan, Rosie and everyone else to hear, "Come and look at Rosie Cotton's Bobby Dazzler! He's a right cockapert! Here young'n. Here Nubby Dux!" She called over to Nathan, hand on her ample hip, "Don'ee let'er slackumtrance go'n 'ticen 'ee away. I'ze pretty mimfy meeself, over 'ere!" She wiggled her hip and fluttered her eyelashes to belching laughter from the others. Rosie heard and stopped. She got her breath back and tried to cool her burning cheeks and look as if she hadn't been sick with worry that they had all left without her. As she came near to Nathan, she saw on his face his struggle between his relief that she had finally arrived, his

169

irritation at her lateness and his urge to appear aloof in front of the villagers. She made an effort to appear as if she hadn't heard the lewd remark of the woman. He stepped back as she approached and promptly slipped in a pile of horse-dung, nearly falling over, arms flailing before he clutched at her arm. The village women cheered coarsely and laughed loudly at his embarrassment.

"I'm sorry, Nathan," Rosie whispered, "I had to wait until my father left until I could get ready. He was again the worse for drink."

"Only just in time." He muttered, trying to scrape the dung off his boot-heel, "Otherwise, we would have to take the hundred and one steps. If your legs were strong enough."

"I've been walking up St. Boniface since I was seven." She reminded him. "Joe and me used to camp up there."

"Well, we'd better get started." Nathan turned towards the cart, muttering under his breath, "And get away from these idiotic peasants as quickly as we can. I am amazed that they have nothing better to do than stand there making fun of us."

Tight-lipped and pale, Nathan helped her into the cart and she took Dickens' hand as he drew her to the place next to him. With a quick angry glance at the woman who had shouted out, Nathan sat down in the cart next to John Leech and stared ahead.

"....and, of course, it might be the physical exercise that is exhausting you, all those rounders and long walks, too many parties, too much gin-punch," Leech was saying to Dickens as the cart lurched off up the lane, "And the emotional drain of Copperfield, writing about Hungerford stairs, your own childhood and its pain, and the feeling of betrayal by your father."

Catching his words, Rosie looked at Leech carefully. His strikingly clear light-blue eyes beneath arcs of heavy dark eyebrows and a large dome of a forehead, a face of extreme sensitivity and amused good-nature, lips firm but ready to smile, set between a large set of mutton-chop whiskers. A good observer, she thought, well able to see beneath the surface of things.

Dickens had brightened slightly as the cart moved off and now leant forward. "John, please let me introduce Miss Rose Cotton and Mister Capper, who is Lord Ashburnham's secretary. Miss Cotton is a writer, too, or soon will be. She has already given me some ideas that I have used." He turned and winked at Rosie. "Rose, this is Mister John Leech, my very good friend, the famous artist, illustrator and cartoonist for Punch Magazine." John Leech bent at the waist, holding onto the back of the jolting cart, "Delighted, Miss Cotton. Very pleased, Mister Capper." He said.

"John has a wicked, though gentle, sense of humour you know. Already, he has put two cartoons of me and my party in Punch whilst we have been here in Bonchurch. One of us being disturbed at a picnic by a wasp," He turned to Rosie, emphasising the strange word with a sly grin, "or *wopse* as you Islanders call it, Miss Cotton, and one, published to my great embarrassment and for all the world to see, of me, the Inimitable, in my shower-bath on the beach!"

"Though suitably and decorously modest - only your head is seen, poking out from behind an invented curtain!" laughed Leech, "My readers couldn't have accepted the awful reality of a naked Dickens in the shower!"

"Can your readers accept the awful reality of anything?" Nathan muttered the question darkly, "Or do you just wish to entertain them with silly pictures?"

They were all shocked by the sudden rudeness of his remark, the acid in it, which had brutally destroyed the light-hearted humour. In the embarrassed pause Rosie watched Nathan tugging at his earlobe. Nobody broke the silence and the unease left by Nathan's comment stayed with them as the carter shouted at the horses, "Bither! Bither!" as the cart turned left up a bend in the steep winding track.

"Bither? What on earth does that mean? I don't like or understand this peasant language..." Nathan looked angrily at Rosie, "...and what does cockapert mean?"

Rosie looked at Nathan coolly. He was clearly agitated by the embarrassment by the pond, trying to cope with the humiliation. She decided to forgive him. "Bither means "turn left" to the horse, and..." She smiled," ...and "cockapert" and "Nubby Dux" means a fancy man, a dandy..."

Nathan looked deeply offended and even more agitated. "Peasants," He said.

They reached the upper slopes. The carter stopped the horses to rest them before the final trudge along the rise to the very top. The unease between the passengers lightened as they all turned to look in different directions at the staggering views. They could see far out into the Channel, spreading like liquid blue glass until lost in the mist and glare of the horizon. Far beneath them, under the very wheels of the cart, the tops of the roofs of the town clustered round Ventnor Cove, like a toy-town, little figures like ants, a flock of gulls squabbling in a cluster of little specks at the end of the new Esplanade, the coal barges moored on the shore, a neat row of white wooden bathing machines - men's at one end, ladies at the other - all perfectly miniature. On the other side the whole of the island spread out fifteen miles to the north and thirty miles west, like a map. They could see Cowes and Ryde and then the Solent channel and Spithead and then, on the other side of the Spithead, eyes squinting in the sunlight, they could see the great sea ports of Southampton and Portsmouth, could even see the thin masts of the crowded ships, like forests in the harbours. "Like flying," thought Rosie, looking down at a small kestrel hovering still in the soft clean breeze below them over the town.

Nathan saw the bird too. "Falco Tinnunculus." He said. "Kestrel."

"Isn't it wonderful?" Rosie gasped, oblivious, "I mean, so high up?"

"Yes, it is." John Leech laughed, leaning forward and thumping Dicken's knee. "Now do you feel better, leaving all your worries down there?" He turned to Nathan beside him, "Feeling better?" He asked kindly, deciding to forgive.

"No. It makes me feel worse, actually. The change in perspective only makes it worse. We all have to go back." Nathan said glumly.

Dickens looked across at him sharply, "What do you mean?"

Nathan's fingers reached for his earlobe and stopped halfway. He put his hand under his thigh and leant forward. "What I mean is that this is just a temporary illusion of escape. We all have to go back."

He sprang up and leapt down from the cart. He stood and pointed out to the Channel. "Over there, just over there, eighty miles away, no more, the great changes have begun. In France, Germany, Italy, Austria, Czechoslovakia, Hungary, in virtually all of the countries of Europe, they have had revolutions to overthrow the cause of their misery. Only last year. And they have succeeded." He turned back to the cart, looking first at Dickens and then at Leech and finally at Rosie. "What you see here is infected. *The way you see it is infected.*"

Funnily, Charles Dickens and John Leech looked as if they understood what Nathan was shouting about. Even the carter had turned in his seat and was staring at Nathan, his brow creased in thought. Rosie forgot to be concerned about not understanding. She started to speak, but the carter got there first.

"What do you'm mean? What use wull't be to louz tha'? How is't be infected, the way we see'n things?"

Nathan reached for a stick on the ground and waved it in the direction of Ryde. The horses flinched and whinnied. "It is infected by her, down there in Osborne House, the German Queen from the house of Hanover.

Her and all her minions and vested interests, landowners, aristocrats, clergymen, the army, the navy, the industrialists, the lawyers, the merchants, and all the others who infest the Great British Beehive and divide it up between them, keeping the vote for themselves, controlling the wealth whilst millions starve to death - not only in Ireland but here, with no help at hand except the hated workhouse. No help."

All four in his audience sat still. All, even Dickens, were spellbound.

"The real toffs. They own everyone and everything. I've read Ashburnham's copy of the Chadwick reports, I have seen the statistics - 500,000 people do not need to work at all and the rest work for them. That is around twelve million workers serving a very small number of very rich people. Over one million people work as domestic servants! Cooking, cleaning, polishing, mopping up, taking orders, cleaning out the horses, cleaning the grates, hoicking coal and great tin bowls of water up endless stairs, emptying piss-buckets - One Million People all day every day, all year every year. But these are the lucky ones. The grain has not grown. Millions are starving, despite the end of the Corn Laws."

"There's no help for the surplus population. They even call us *the surplus population* openly, we have even begun to believe it ourselves, that we ourselves are surplus according to natural law, that death is natural for us because we are surplus to economic requirements!" Nathan had started to scream, but then his voice suddenly fell. "Because we are not profitable." He looked at Dickens, "just like your baby farm." He sneered softly,

"They have created a reality for us, a big fragile mirror that looks like reality and they yearly spend vast sums of money keeping it well polished and in place. They tell us that we should look to God for help, stopping us looking at them too closely, stopping us from looking behind the mirror at the real things."

Dickens and the carter began to speak up. This time Dickens won. "You've been reading Karl Marx, haven't you? The Communist Manifesto?"

Nathan stopped laughing. "Once you see through it, you can see the cant in everything. In the sermons, in the attitudes, in the narrowness of people and their complacency, locked in the jail of this mental creation they have built for us."

"But surely some things are true, like sermons, like good and evil?" Objected Rosie.

"What? Like your Readings for Every Day in Lent, I suppose? No. Nothing will change by reading those good books. It is nothing more that cynical manipulation to keep you docile, don't you understand? We can only find the truth by smashing the mirror." Nathan flung the stick hard out into the air above Ventnor and they watched it slowly fall through the big air and disappear beneath them. Nathan turned back and looked at Rosie. "You, dear, sweet Rosie. You are a truly beautiful creature, untainted by this world because you live at the very edge of it. But when you begin to get sucked in, you will find that there are no such things as good and evil. Most things lie buried in the grey sludge between them. Is it so truly evil for a starving man to poach a rabbit to feed his children? Yet for this he can be deported. This is the law of the rich. And it doesn't have to be like this."

He turned toward Dickens, "You, you sentimentalist. You think that by writing about the miseries of the underworld and the poor you engage the sentiment of the masses. But by doing this, you accept it, you reinforce it, you perpetuate it, you make money from it." He picked up a bigger stick and the nearest horse flinched again. Rosie saw the horse tense its hind legs and raise and drop them together in the dust.

The carter tipped his hat back on his head, "Hey you! Now doan't go annearst the mare, account of she might fling at ye, see."

John Leech sprang to his feet in a rage. "How dare you?! You insult the nation's greatest author!" He shouted, "A great artist!" But Dickens pulled him back to his seat and held him back. "Wait." He spoke quietly, with authority. He looked down at Nathan and Rosie saw sadness in his large grave eyes. Then he smiled grimly. "I know something about poverty and desperation and betrayal. And I understand the damage it causes, because I live with it inside me all the time." He looked at John Leech. "Yes, you know that I do, John." He turned back to Nathan, "And I think that I understand you and I also think that what you say has some truth in it."

Nathan looked at Dickens and then he nodded. "Urania Cottage." He swallowed. "My sister was there. Alice. She knew you, Mister Dickens."

"Alice Capper. Yes, I remember. A poor girl. We couldn't help her." Dickens shrugged. "So disfigured by the acid burn. We tried. But when it was healed, the scars grown over, she left us. Just like that. She joined the missionaries and went abroad."

"China. She was sent to China."

"Do you hear anything of her?"

"Not a thing….."

Dickens looked at John Leech. "It was a double tragedy. Alice was a fallen woman – a young girl from the Holy Land - who we took in to our home at Urania Cottage in the clean air and green fields of Shepherds Bush outside the capital. But her determination to reform angered her pimp who took his revenge in a dose of sulphuric acid. It nearly killed her."

Dickens looked at Rosie, "Be careful with this young man," He murmured, "He is dangerous. He has the raw honesty and outrage of youth. Thank God for our youth and the outrage. It is the future." He looked at Nathan again, "But what can you do after your fine speech?" He asked gently, "What do you see in your future?"

Nathan walked in front of the horses and squinted up at Dickens and the carter, pulling at his ear. "All I can tell you is that in the full eighteen months since my sister Alice was taken in by the missionaries, I have thought of nothing, nothing but taking a mallet to the glass of false reality. I, we, are going to smash the mirror." He took two steps forward and hurled the big stick up in the air. "Smash it!" He yelled.

Rosie knew what was going to happen as soon as she saw the horses' eyes widen and roll and their ears go back. As Nathan let his arm back to hurl the stick, both horses leapt forward straight at him, jerking the heavy cart forward. She saw Nathan go down under their hooves as she shot back along the cart's bench. Dickens slid off the bench onto the floor of the cart and nearly fell out. John Leech managed to grip the sides and stay in his place. "Whoa, Whoa!" The carter drew the horses up and leapt down, peering under the cart, muttering, deep lines of worry in his brow, "I'll ginnee a girt leatherin' for this hyster for long, you daft hoss." He slowly straightened and looked up at his passengers, "He's astrout unerneath."

"Underneath? Oh God," Rosie clambered off the back of the cart. "Mister Dickens, Mister Leech! He's underneath! How are we going to find a doctor?"

The carter held on to the horses while Leech and Dickens dragged Nathan out from underneath the cart. He was unconscious. Dickens knelt and tore at Nathan's scarf and collar buttons, "Quick, John, help me get his jacket off and carry him into the shade of that gorse. Rosie, could you kneel down with his head in your lap please?"

Rosie did so as Dickens and John Leech carried Nathan into the shade and laid him out so that his head was supported on Rosie's knees. Dickens threw off his own jacket and knelt by her, rolling up his sleeves, flexing and stretching his fingers. "Now, I want nobody to say anything until I tell you." Dickens closed his eyes and breathed deeply for a few moments. Then he splayed his fingers, relaxed his hands and with supreme concentration and gentleness began to move his palms in the shapes of caresses, following the line of Nathan's head, never more than two inches from the skin and hair. He looked up at Rosie. "Don't be alarmed, Rosie," He murmured, speaking slowly and quietly, "It's called

179

animal magnetism. I am letting the invisible magnetic fluid flow out of my fingertips into Nathan's head and body, redistributing his own magnetic energy and restoring the balance of it." He paused as his hands coasted the air over Nathan's scalp, then continued in the tones of afterthought, with extreme precision and quietness, concentrating.

He stopped moving his hands. "Nathan. Nathan. Can you hear me?" Rosie heard a new cadence in his voice, a fresh vibration. Distilled caring, she thought, he speaks with distilled caring.

"Nathan? Can you hear me?"

Nathan's eyes fluttered in his pale face and then opened, looked at Dickens, locked onto his eyes, "Yes, I can hear you." He spoke slowly, as if the words came from deep within him, taking their time to float up to the surface.

"Nathan, where does it hurt?"

"In my head....."

"Nathan. Please look into my eyes. There. Now please sleep." Dickens rested both of his palms lightly on Nathan's head, his voice now little more than a whisper. "You are asleep now. And I am curing your pain. And you will help me. Look at the pain in your head, see its shape and colour. You are helping me are you not?"

"Yes. I am helping you."

"What shape and colour is the pain in your head?"

"Like flint. A shard of flint, silver and sharp ...." Nathan's face winced.

A pause. "Look at it Nathan. And the pain will go. It is receding, is it not?"

"It is receding."

Still Dickens kept his hands in place, and after another pause murmured again, the words clear and distinct, "The pain has gone now, has it not?"

"Yes, it has gone."

"Nathan. I want you to sleep for a little longer and then wake up and you will be completely better. Cured of your pain. Do you understand me?"

"I understand, but the ship ......"

Dickens looked up at Rosie, startled. She shrugged. She knew of no ship, nor had Nathan ever mentioned one to her. Dickens looked down at Nathan's face. "What is it that you wish to tell me about the ship, Nathan?"

"The ship. It is coming. I must be ready. I have a great deal to do."

Dickens decided it was unimportant. "Please do not worry about the ship."

"But I must be ready. The ship is coming. It will be here."

"Calm yourself, Nathan, there is time. Now I want you to come awake." He paused. "Now."

Nathan's eyes opened and stared for a moment uncomprehendingly at Dickens, then up at Rosie's face, then at John Leech and the carter standing anxiously behind Dickens. They pulled him to his feet and Rosie helped him put on his jacket before he climbed unsteadily into the back of the cart. Dickens turned to the carter. "Would you please take Mr. Capper down to the Bonchurch Tap at Ribbands Hotel and inform the innkeeper and Lord Ashburnham of what has taken place? Mr. Capper must see a doctor as soon as he arrives, of course. We will walk the rest of the way."

As the carter turned back to send his whip over the horses, the men looked after the receding cart uneasily, with quiet thought.

Then John Leech bent down and picked something up from the ground. "Look, Charles. This must have fallen from his pocket as he fell." It was a book, left in the grass. He slowly read out the title. *"On the Treatment and Management of the Insane, with Considerations on Public and Private Lunatic Asylums.* By Doctor Millingen. Four shillings and sixpence,"* He put the book in his pocket. "I'll leave it with the inn-keeper at his lodgings..."

"Do you think poor Nathan Capper is going mad? I wonder why he suddenly mentioned a ship? I have never known anything like that happen before....usually when I do this, the patient just wakes up when I say so." Rosie heard the slight irritation in Dickens's voice.

Leech shrugged, "Imagination?"

"Not at all. It's the imagination which is the welding force which enables magnetism to work. I believe that I have enough imagination always to make it work, as long as the patient believes in it or can be brought to believe in it. But no, at that level in his mind, whatever he says about the ship was, is, definitely real. No, John, his anxiety about that ship is embedded deep in his mind. It must be something very important to him. Something urgent."

Rosie listened, shocked and feeling suddenly sick. She remembered the noise of Nathan's angry speech. She felt that he was dangerous. She felt that he had gone beyond her reach. He was isolated, closed up, obsessive, driven. She was so unsettled by Nathan's outburst that she had hardly noticed the printed blue envelope with the curious design, glimpsed in Nathan's inner pocket as she had risen, stiff-kneed, and helped Nathan put on his jacket. Now, as she thought about it, she remembered where she had seen that envelope before.

The envelope was exactly the same envelope which she had seen James Wiskard waving at her father with such force in the garden of East Dene Manor.

The ship was another mystery.

23

Rosie put the candlestick on the earth floor and stared out of the window. There was no moon. But as her eyes adjusted to the dim starlight she could just make out the dark shape of the two-masted brigantine which had come in under nightfall, now riding at anchor without lights. Her father had rowed out to meet it and had returned to shore with a group of men. She hadn't seen them clearly, but knew that two remained on the beach, hidden amongst the rocks, as look-outs. Their accents had been different from the local accent of the Island. As her father had directed, Rosie filled the two jugs three-quarters with ale and topped them up with spirit. She then twice raised the candle at the side window and stood waiting at the door.

As she waited, she thought about Nathan. Ever since he had disappeared in the back of the cart over the side of the hill on the downs she hadn't seen him at all. Nathan had vanished, but his speech had remained with her and its effect had been immediate. When Charles Dickens and John Leech and she had eventually arrived at the picnic, the minute she was told, more than asked, to help ladling out the boiled potatoes, the cold meat and the salads, she had begun to see Nathan's words being played out in front of her by the small group of people there. The deference shown by the women to the men, their acceptance of the clergymen's empty patter, the clergymen's deference to the rich and to the famous. She began to see the structure of their relationships clearly. Once begun, this new awareness had grown and now she saw it everywhere she looked. Relationships were based on wealth. She began to understand what Nathan had meant, began to recognise herself and her reflection in his mirror, her place defined by the attitudes of the people about her.

She had tried to return to her everyday life as before, but she now realised that Nathan had infected her with this new awareness and, because of it, return was impossible. Saturday, 19th September 1849 had come and had gone. Bargain Saturday had gone for another year. And she had not gone to Newport. She no longer wanted the life of a scullery maid in a farmhouse. She was not certain what she wanted, but she knew she would not have been able to put up with that.

There was change in the air, but change had not yet visibly come. But one incident in the old church broke the pattern. Each Sunday, the Rector's sermon had grown noisier and angrier than the last, his rage filling the tiny space as he stood on the tiles, legs akimbo before his small flock which stood back as far as possible, giving him the remaining space, pressed against the walls in a solid crush before him, as he told of the latest enormity which deserved his wrath. It all seemed to do with money. She felt anxious all the time these days. There was anxiety in the air, it seemed, as well as change. The coastline was emerging on all fronts from obscurity to a notoriety.

"Some say it is another El Dorado." The Rector had begun with the low voice of warning, "It is not", he shouted, his face suffused purple. Rosie had seen all the frantic activity with her own eyes, as every day she had walked through the streets of the new town being thrown up at Ventnor, higgling her crabs, weaving between the armies of uncouth labourers and the great carts of sawn stone careering down from the quarries and the timber hauled up from the barges on the shore, all the time trying to keep her feet and dress out of the slop and swill of the deep mud.

"It is nothing less than Mammon itself. It is pure, unadulterated greed! Speculators without capital or credit! Builders without skill or the most basic competence, armies of the worst sort of low life swarming like ants in from the mainland cities, to crawl over the carcasses of their ungodly creations, thrown up without planning, without sanitation in Ventnor and now even in Sandown Bay." The Rector paused and then, unbelievably, pointed his finger across the heads of the Respectable, directly at James Wiskard who sat cramped in one of the front pews. "Greed based on a financial expectation," He thundered, "Will be the ruin of us all!"

The congregation had frozen, silent, as the two men faced each other across the narrow space. No pew-door creaked, no cushion shifted, no boot scraped. James Wiskard scratched his beard, put on his bowler hat, gathered his bulk and squeezed it past the other occupants of the pew-stall, opened the pew door and walked out.

Rosie was jerked out of her memories as the cottage door opened and one of the men off the brigantine stood there waiting for the jugs. He took a noisy swig as he received them, "Ah. Elixir! Ay-licks-eeyer!" He pronounced the long vowels slowly with relish, "Even better than the Cornish, I truly declare." He grinned down at her. "You'll have to show me the way after we get to the top of the cliff."

So they were from Cornwall, far away along the mainland coast! Rosie couldn't understand why they should have come all this way for twenty-odd tubs of spirit; surely there was easy trade enough with the French in Cornwall. As she led the way up the track in front of the Cornishman, she saw from the corner of her eye the quick flash of a spout lantern pointed towards the moored barque. Careless! she thought. If used properly, the beam from the long tin spout at the front could only be seen from those at whom it was directed. Everyone knew it was illegal to signal from the shore. It was even breaking the law to carry a lantern along the coast.

She waited at the top of the cliff for a few moments, to make as sure as she could that nobody apart from the signaller lurked in the darkness. Once certain, Rosie motioned to the Cornishman to follow and scrambled over a stile under the trees and through the long field up to the orchard by the ruined cottage.

Without a moon she found it difficult to find the exact spot in the short grass at the base of the wall. When she did, she took a stone and rapped three times on the slab and waited until it was moved aside from below. Her father's white hair showed in the dark as his head emerged from the hole, he silently took hold of one jug and motioned the Cornishman down the spiral steps in front of him.

"Go home, Rosie, and go to sleep!" Her father growled in her ear, "It's more than your life's worth to get mixed up in this." With that, he descended the stairwell and drew the stone slab across the hole above him.

Rosie hesitated in the darkness, her heart beating. This was different from the usual simple collection and run of tubs over the top of St. Boniface Down and down into the centre of the Island to Rookley. She must find out what was happening. She could sneak in through the other side, she thought, but they would have placed hidden guards all around and, if she was caught sneaking in, her father would take the rope to her with a vengeance for disobeying his order. Then, in a flash, she remembered it! There was a second tunnel! Joe's Secret Passage.

Joe had discovered it in the cellar of the ruined cottage by the orchard, when he was a very young boy. He had sworn her to absolute secrecy before telling her about it. She remembered with an ache how she and Joe had played there and how she had been touched and awed by the importance in his bearing as he gravely led her down into the dark cellar of the cottage, and the high clear tones of his voice as he forced her to put her hand on her heart, and again to swear secrecy.

He had pulled an old wooden chest away from the wall and shown her the rusty iron grating behind it, hinged to give access to the perfectly round stone tunnel. "It's my secret passage, Rosie," He declared as he went into the dark, "We'll call it Joe's Secret Passage!" She had been too scared to go in but had waited for Joe to reappear, sick with worry for his safety.

This time, older, she managed to control her terror at the black hole. The chest was still there and she moved it aside with ease. The grating stuck a bit but she got it open. She would have given anything to have Joe with her. Remembering her vow of secrecy even now, she pulled the grating shut behind her, and through the bars hauled the chest back against it as far as she could. She was in pitch black. She couldn't see her hand in front of her face. In the musty stillness the only sound was the rasp of her breathing. With a colossal exertion of will-power Rosie finally let go of the grating. In the blackness, she imagined Joe leading her along. He was simple to conjure up in her mind, his bright yellow hair and a big smile, so real that she could almost touch the rough cloth and shiny brass buttons of his jacket. Praying for a piece of his courage, she began to feel her way, gingerly groping the smooth curve of the stone, into the closeness.

The air became more dense and fusty. Rosie forced herself to remember that all she had to do was return along the tunnel to reach the surface. She had no idea how long she had been moving when she suddenly heard a sharp scrape, to one side above her head. Her fingers on the wall felt an empty space and the air became fresher. She stopped. Yes, she could definitely hear their voices. Timidly, she moved into the empty space and felt a downward draught. Her exploring fingers felt the wall on the other side of the space. Joe hadn't mentioned a side-passage, she remembered, undecided whether to continue.

Turning into the space, her toe stubbed on a stone. She bent down, stretching her fingers out, and felt the edge of a step, another steeply above it and then another, raking up. She began to climb.

It seemed endless. She had silently counted twenty steps when she was presented with an extraordinary sight. Through a stone grill, she looked down over a ledge into the body of a small hall, lit by several smoking tallow candles. She could see more than twenty men lounging on old oak chairs. She recognised the local fishermen on the far side and, amongst the strangers immediately below her, she saw the man who had carried the jugs. The two jugs stood on the floor, by the legs of one. The legs looked familiar. The man stood up suddenly and looked around the rest of the gathering, caught in the candlelight. It was James Wiskard.

His wheezing voice was clearly audible to her in the silence. "We must do it. We have no choice!" He cried out.

"No choice!" repeated the echo from the walls around Rosie's head. Startled, James Wiskard looked up quickly. To her terror, he seemed to look straight up at her. He paused, one of his eyes meeting hers through the grill. For a moment, she believed that he had seen her. But his expression remained unchanged, and he dropped his head and looked back across the hall, lowering his voice. "I tell you that if we don't, we'll all be bankrupt and all our properties will be taken by the lawyers and the banks. This dream town we're creating, it's built on bits of worthless paper, and when the final reckoning comes - *when someone actually demands real payment in hard cash -then we'll find that nobody has any.* We'll all be grabbing the small change we have left and waving Promissory Notes and

I.O.U's signed by each other. We'll all suffer, especially our dear brother here."

Rosie looked where he was pointing, at a figure sitting well back in the last pew under a pillar and stifled her gasp of amazement only just in time. Wiskard was pointing at the Rector! The shocking reality hit Rosie and she wanted to scream. They were all in it together! What was it they were planning?

She only heard the last part of Wiskard's next sentence," sold off all of his land bit by bit to pay his debts, like all you other so-called gentility."

Rosie recognised the faces of others of the local gentry in the group. The Rector stood up, quivering. "Yes, and we sold to whom? Mainly to you, Wiskard, and I am going to collect!"

Wiskard's hoarse voice rose with impatience. "You never did listen, did you, you flustergating cushion-thumper! All you do is shake like a jelly, go beetroot, point fingers and pontificate! You're a damn fool if you think you'll get any money from me if we don't go through with this to the hilt!" His eyes in the candlelight looked inflamed, one circling in its socket, the other glaring red at the Rector, "I can't even pay my quarry men, masons and labourers. We're all waiting for payment from Baron this and Lady that!" His voice reached its pitch with exasperation, " I tell you, dear brother," He sneered, "You can wait no longer!"

"Wait no longer," Came a mournful echo.

Another voice calmly interceded with quiet lacerating authority, icily cutting through the bombast and heat. "The ship will be here within three days and I and my men will take a full quarter of the gold and silver as payment."

To Rosie, the temperature seemed to drop. She looked around, trying to see who had spoken. Out of the shadows at the corner of the hall and into its centre slowly strolled a very big man. As he stood beneath the pulpit, even in the dim candlelight, Rosie could see his bright red hair under a black floppy tarpaulin hat. He stood, perfectly at ease, like a huge predator before its prey, facing the daunted group. "That's settled then."

Rosie noticed that, despite his crystal enunciation, his voice had a curiously rich quality to it, pleasing to the ear, as if it came from inside a wooden barrel. "Gentlemen, I guarantee that your financial worries are over. My young friend here will tell you the name of the ship in due course." The big man beckoned to a figure in the darkness and into the centre of the floor stepped Nathan Capper.

Rosie's mind froze as she grasped the cold stone and watched Nathan. He stood looking at them all diffidently and then reached into his pocket and drew out the blue envelope. "I have here details of the method of converting the treasure into banknotes through a series of receivers and fences in London and Amsterdam. All the arrangements are in place. The value will be discounted of course, as each receiver takes his cut. It will take no more than one month to complete," Nathan looked around the group and smiled, "I hope no more than two weeks. For this service, I will be paid a fee of one tenth of the total resultant monies. This will be used to fund the revolutionary brotherhood." He paused, looking around at each face, "I must remind you that we are all in this together and that both trust and secrecy are of the essence."

Nathan followed the big man as he walked towards a door at the back of the hall. The big man suddenly stopped and turned, "One more thing. Young Nathan here has said it right. But I just want to add a little emphasis. If any of you betray me, any single one of you," As he looked slowly across them, seeming to pause momentarily at each one, Rosie caught in the candlelight, across the empty space between them, the startling brightness of his green eyes, "I'll slaughter him and every member of his entire family, so help me God."

To Rosie, transfixed high up behind the grill, the echo of his footsteps and the slam of the door seemed to hang in the air long after he and his men had left.

She saw her father get to his feet and walk across to James Wiskard, putting an arm across his shoulders, a complacent smirk on his lips, playing the reassuring middleman. "We're in, then," he said, "It's settled."

She saw the Rector go to the door, followed quickly by the other gentlemen. Rosie's father gestured to the fisherman standing guard, "It's all right. Let 'em go," He ordered.

Rosie turned to descend the steps. She was no longer afraid of the tunnel. Her mind was in turmoil, trying to understand what it meant. The ship that the big man had spoken of. What were they going to do when it arrived? All she could think of was that it might be a big smuggling run. But then, thinking of her father's words, she knew it had to be something deeper, something much more sinister - something that made it more than her life was worth to know about.

PART EIGHT

24

Alice

For Alice, the ship was a monster. A great creaking wooden machine which could never rest, never stay still. Its cobwebs of ropes confused her, the height of the masts frightened her, the endless ringing of the bell every half-hour deprived her of sleep and the crew was now avoiding her, their earlier respect having evaporated. She had found a place out of the wind amidships which rocked least and by keeping her eyes fixed on the horizon managed to hold down the sickness which she had suffered since leaving Hong Kong harbour.

For Alice, a girl, the only female on board, it was hell. Decorum was difficult, if not impossible. The toilet was placed in the bow just above the water line. Slots cut near the floor level allowed the wave action to wash it out. Only the captain had a private toilet near his quarters, at the stern of the ship. She had first tried the bow, seeking privacy, choosing her moment carefully, squatting, arms gripping the damp woodwork, as she crashed up and down in the bow, unable to bring herself to perform.

Constipated, sick, she had finally found the opportunity for a quiet word with the doctor.

His alarm evident, he was profuse in apology, his Irish accent laden with remorse.

"My God, I should have thought about this before, I'm so sorry Miss Capper, I'll have a word with Captain Doe. We are not used to having a woman aboard. We cannot let you fall sick."

He was kind, but practical. "Contagion would destroy the crew. We must take care of you for all our sakes."

She was allowed to use the Captain's toilet, but then the averted gazes of the crew, the smirks, the too careful politeness as she emerged, marked her out, she thought to herself, as being a useless piece of baggage reluctantly carried by the men in their closed world of the sailing machine.

And then she felt the blood seeping between her legs.

25

No clean cloths. No private washing facilities. Few changes of clothes. Desperate, Alice found the doctor. As she sat on a wooden chest in his tiny cabin, knees pressed together, she felt the blood flow thicken.

"I'll have to examine you."

In the face of her ordeal, all remains of modesty disappeared. Alice was too tired to resist or object. It had to be done. After all, she had been a whore for her own survival in the Holy Land. She had been used to men looking at her body before the scalding of the acid. The missionaries and their easy answers, their promise of salvation after death, had offered a means of escape, no more. Her life was a ruin. Now she needed help.

The doctor locked the cabin door and helped her undress, the blood-stained clothes dropping to the floor. He took a clean dry sponge and dropped it into a pail of water.

"It's been boiled, so it's clean," He muttered as he very gently wiped her vagina and her upper thighs, "I have more dry sponges which you must wear until the monthly cycle is done."

The gentle touch of his fingers, his mellow voice, the tiny warm cabin, the selfless intimacy. Alice had never known such kindness. The blood-stained garments on the floor of the cabin, the years of tightly-grasped reserve she had wrapped around her soul were willingly forsaken. She felt tears press her eyelids and then well up, and began to cry. She put her arms around his neck and kissed the top of his head, "Thank you."

"No, please." The doctor stood and moved back. "Please put on clean clothes, Miss Capper."

His professional reprimand brought her back. The moment was gone.

"I think that it is best," The doctor's voice lowered as he tried to contain his sexual excitement, "That we'll have to try to get you off this ship, Miss Capper."

26

After Pendleton's ship had gone beneath the horizon, after the refusal to transfer Alice off the Sea Witch, Alice began to give up, resigned to the months at sea before they would reach England. She stopped being sick, stopped trying to cover her face in the wind. Her scars darkened in the sun. She felt disembodied, sailing the empty seas. Abandoned, she was losing her fragile faith. The missionaries' teachings evaporated from her mind as she tried to hold onto them in the face of the indifference of the huge sky and the endless water.

But something had changed. The doctor was her friend. He was warm, honest, kind, funny, protective. He didn't seem to notice her scars. She felt free with him. Free of pretence. She began to feel that he genuinely cared for her.

One evening, the ship rolling quietly under a soft breeze south along the coast of East Africa, the doctor had held her hand as they stood on the aft deck out of sight of the sailors. With a small shock, Alice sensed the strength of their togetherness, the loneliness she had felt all of her life blown over the side by the breeze and the new warmth she felt.

PART NINE

27

Jane Tench

"I really hope they do fresh milk as well as tinned food and pasta?"

"Food banks are basics only. You get what they got." Fiona shrugged, "We might be lucky."

Fiona had given me one of the old sandwiches from her waitress job, but I was still starving. We had run out of coffee.

Fiona had made me change into my oldest clothes to "look the part". She ruffled my hair. I pulled out a pair of old scuffed walking boots and left the laces untied.

We reached a small brick building squeezed between two shops. A large faded sign above the door proclaimed that it was the Ventnor Spiritualist Church. It didn't look at all like a church, more like an old warehouse. Inside, the place was bigger than I had expected, and I was surprised to see that it was packed, all the way to the back. It didn't look good and there was no sign of any food bank.

A lady at the door welcomed us with a bright smile, gave us each a book and told Fiona that she had specially saved us a place at the front. Fiona led me forward down the narrow aisle, struggled past the people sitting in the chairs, saying hello right and left. All were very friendly and excited, as if they were there to see a show.

"Got to do this, see?" Fiona whispered in my ear, "Otherwise no food bank."

I looked around. They were all ages, most were old ladies with perms and elaborately-shaped and brightly-coloured glasses which magnified their eyes alarmingly as they caught my gaze, but also younger women of my age and men both young and old, seemingly absorbed in self-conscious reflection.

"Are they all really here for the food?" My stomach was beginning to cramp.

"Sshh. It's just something we have to go through."

In front there was a simple platform and a long raised bench in ornate woodwork, over which two faces looked down calmly at the assembled crowd. One stood up and the room immediately fell quiet with expectation.

"Friends, welcome!" He spoke with a gentle authority, "It is wonderful to see so many of you today, and especially heart-warming to see the popularity of our friend, Roderick, the celebrated medium and accomplished clairvoyant, who I'm sure will give us further evidence of survival of the spirit after death, in which we all believe." He gestured to the other face, whose owner then stood up. Roderick was short and didn't look at all as I had imagined a clairvoyant to be. He looked more like an accountant, with neatly trimmed brown hair, a smart suit and tie and a large pair of spectacles resting on his button-nose.

"Friends, Roderick would like us to sing a hymn and say a prayer before he makes contact with the Other Side," A tiny frail lady perched expectantly on a stool in the corner in front of a small electric organ. Immediately, the vigorous music swelled through the amplifier and the crowd launched into the song with gusto. I joined in, infected by hunger. Singing seemed to reduce my discomfiture. I was desperately trying not to fart.

As the music finished and a prayer commenced, I was struck by the tone of their voices as they prayed. It sounded as if they were really talking to somebody; most unlike the dreary repetition that I had heard in a proper church. As the last verse of the prayer faded, the audience sat. Roderick remained standing behind the wooden bench, his eyes shut tightly behind his glasses.

There was a long pause in the silence of the packed room. And then Roderick started to murmur, almost to himself.....

"I have something............" He had a lisping voice, strongly coloured with a lilting Welsh accent, "Something towards the back, over there..." His eyes still shut, his arm raised limply and he motioned towards the left of the room, away from us, "A Dorothy...." Roderick opened his eyes, "For you Madam, there, over there, yes! You Madam, I have a Dorothy! Do you, please, have a Dorothy on the Spirit Plane?" I turned to look as a young woman began to nod, her eyes wide, flushed with excitement.

"She's showing me flowers.... she's laughing, she's saying they were a waste when she died, you gave her all those flowers, huge bunches covering the grave," Roderick paused, his head tilted, listening to a voice which only he could hear, "She says she loves flowers; she looked down at you all gathered at the funeral and saw you all.... George? Dorothy is telling me that you have a brother called George?

The young woman didn't seem perturbed by this at all. In a calm voice she called out firmly and clearly over the heads of the others, "Yes! Dorothy is my mother and George is my brother."

"Well, she says that George is not to worry so much about his exams.... that all of his hard work will pay off... that she loves both of you very much and... are you a painter, Miss, an artist? - You don't mind if I call you Miss, do you? Dorothy tells me that you're not married...." A ripple of amusement broke out. The young woman laughed and called out again, "I am a painter and I'm not married; and I will tell George not to worry! Thank you very much."

"She's showing me some red shoes, some bright red shoes.... please, do you have a pair of bright red shoes? Maybe in a painting? In a portrait of someone? Yes! That's it! The shoes are in a painting you're doing now. Is that correct?"

I looked back at the woman, shocked to see that she was now in tears, her shoulders hunched and quivering with grief. But she kept her head raised; the tears there openly for all to see. The atmosphere was electric. Nobody moved. The two people either side of the girl left her alone, looking straight ahead, respecting her dignity. Taking her time, the girl managed the same clarity of voice despite her tears, "I am painting a portrait of my mother from a photograph taken before she died...." She swallowed hard, a sudden clench of grief interrupting her, "Yes, she had red shoes.... and I am having difficulty getting the shoes right in the painting. Everything else is perfect, but I've tried repainting the shoes about, Oh gosh! About seven or eight times!" She suddenly laughed through her tears.

There was a pause, Roderick was listening again. I listened too. Everyone in the room was listening. Listening out for Dorothy.

At last Roderick spoke, his voice resonating with the love held in Dorothy's words, "She says... my dear, Dorothy says.... that she waits for you on the Other Side and that she loves you and will watch over you on the Physical Plane until you join her....that you will have a long and happy life. Even that you will soon be married to a man whom you will love till you die and, and, she says .... she says do not change the red shoes, don't change them. Leave them as they are. Please, Dorothy loves them that way. She says because.... because," Roderick bent his head to the voice in his ears, "She says whenever you look at them now, you will remember this conversation that we are having and will know that she is alive in spirit ...and will remember that she will always love you." Roderick nodded, "She is leaving now. God bless you."

There was absolute stillness in the room, all of us moved by the beauty of the words. The girl's face glowed.

Roderick straightened up, his eyes closed again, "Over here! Now over here!" His arm arched, his finger pointing over the waiting heads, descending until it pointed straight at me. My stomach lurched. I looked at Fiona who smiled at me reassuringly. I looked at the old lady in the next seat on the other side, hoping it would be her turn next, that Roderick didn't mean me. I smelt a strong odour of lavender water. "....A loss, a recent feeling of loss... of losing....," Roderick's eyes opened behind his spectacles. There was no doubt. He was looking at me. "Not a physical loss, an emotional loss. Please, young lady, yes there. Have you felt a loss recently?" Roderick waited, waiting for my answer and at the same time listening to voices from another world.

To my amazement, I found my voice, "Yes I have," I sounded surprisingly calm, I thought, as I acknowledged the question, "A relationship..........ended badly."

"I can see fear. There's a reprisal coming. Danger...danger to your life. A dark evil. Revenge is coming. But I see hope."

I swallowed noisily, the tension in my gut beginning to hurt.

"....Mmh, Mmh....I am seeing a picture....lights, coloured lights in a row. And flags hung up, waving in the breeze. It's dark, but I can see it all clearly. It's the moon! It's a full moon! And... and I can hear the sea, not distantly but all around, all around.... but I am not in the sea or even in a boat. It's the pier! I'm on the end of the pier! There's a man standing there, in the moonlight at the end of the pier.... in the moonlight. He feels like, like.... He's wearing a sort of uniform with a peaked cap. Now he's crouching. He's crouching down against the railing at the end of the pier. He's covering his ears, fists in his ears...."

I could feel Fiona looking sideways at me, feel her disturbance, a strange gnawing fear beginning to grow in my mind.

"A voice! He's saying something about a voice, He's saying he's saying....that a voice will come. The voice will come to you!" Roderick suddenly staggered to one side, seized, hunched. Then, as if hit by an electric current, he stretched upward, arms straining out, his fingers clawing the air, *"It's a warning!"* He screamed, *"It's a warning!* You must beware the voice when it comes to you! Don't listen! You must not listen ...when, when" His voice trailed off to silence.

" When I speak to you"

Roderick had changed. His voice had changed. His arms had dropped to his side. He stood entranced, lifeless. Roderick had gone. They were now hearing another. The frozen audience sat like stone figures, powerless to intervene, nailed by horror. The voice that came out of Roderick's mouth was as hard and bright as flint. Female without doubt, but with a stark power which invaded the room by natural right, filling it, penetrating everyone's minds with a cold intent.

"You know where I am found. I await you. This midnight. Farewell."

The voice had gone. The spirit had left, leaving a chasm of empty silence in the room. Roderick's body slumped forward and slid from sight behind the wooden bench.

In the pandemonium that followed, Fiona managed to pull me out of a side door. Someone was yelling for an ambulance. The organist had fainted.

PART TEN

28

Rosie sat with a candle, alone in the comer of her cottage, listening to the howl of the September gale outside, scratching a steel nib across some old newspapers, dipping it into the black ink held in Nathan's inkstands, drawing patterns. She couldn't write her verses, the words wouldn't come or wouldn't scan. And her mind too full. She was chilled by the change in her father. He hadn't drunk a drop of grog for three days. But a frightening new side to him had emerged now he was sober. Before, he had hardly seemed aware of her existence, except when she had failed to perform some menial task. Now, he watched her. He contrived to find out everywhere she went and who she spoke to. He had stopped her from higgling. She felt closed in, aware of an approaching danger but unable to fully understand what it was, like a mouse under the eye of the circling kestrel. Then, two days before, he had forbidden her to go any further than to the falling stream for water. Rosie knew that the plan that she had seen them all agree to was about to take place, but she still had no way of knowing what their plan was.

She dared not ask about the ship or the big Cornishman with red hair and she had learned nothing more. She knew that if she asked, her father would suspect that she knew more than she was supposed to.

She kept her silence, noticing only that her father now seemed to walk with a swagger and seemed to have plenty of money which had appeared from nowhere. It must be something to do with the plan, with the ship that she had heard the big Cornishman mention and now she knew it must be the same ship which Dickens had unlocked in Nathan's mind. Once, when she was walking past the old church with her father, they had met the Rector as he emerged from the evening service and Rosie had been struck by the way the Rector had looked all about him carefully before speaking to her father. Even more surprising to her had been the Rector's manner, the way he deferred to her father's authority, greeting him as more than an equal and listening to her father's brief words with the automatic, unquestioning attention of an underdog, as if to a master. It amazed Rosie to find that her father had naturally adopted the tone and posture of authority, the social roles completely reversed, and she wondered what power her father could have over the Rector which made the churchman so obsequious. Applying Nathan's theory and what she had heard, she knew that it must involve huge wealth.

She couldn't help being amused at the sight of the pompous Rector now almost cringing at the feet of the fisherman, but at the same time she knew with a feeling of uneasy disquiet that the thing which had caused such a radical reversal must be sinister. The two had turned the Nathan's mirror round between them and Rosie had seen a glimpse of the scratches in the silvering behind. It made her nervous and unsettled. Those scratches would only get bigger.

The door crashed open, letting the rough night in. Her father came through the door drenched by the gale outside, hunched over some large parcels and carrying a wicker hamper in the other hand. Kicking the door shut against the storm, he threw the parcels at her feet and dumped the hamper on the thin wooden table. With a flourish, he ripped open the lid and, item by item naming each one in turn, ceremoniously brought out delicacies which she had never seen before - cold roasted turkey, rich warm russet french wines in bottles with ornate labels, asparagus, roast potatoes - all prepared and packed with white linen napery, cut glass goblets and solid silver cutlery. There were even two elaborately-carved silver candlesticks. There were three goblets.

He laughed at her disbelieving face. Then he reached down, ripped open one of the parcels and pulled out a gown of bright blue silk and some new leather ladies' shoes, some earrings and a pearl necklace and told her to put them on, wash her face and brush her hair.

Speechless, Rosie obeyed. As she washed hurriedly in the clay basin in the corner, she decided that it was either to do with the big man from Cornwall and the arrival of the ship or just maybe, the thought made her heart leap, maybe that her father knew that Joe was coming home and hadn't told her.

Certainly, it was almost inconceivable that he would go to all these lengths, but Rosie was so sure that Joe was near that she could easily believe it now. For the past three days, she had dreamt of Joe every night, had seen him walking the deck of a ship, had heard the crack and strain of the rigging and felt the strong breeze, as if she was standing next to him on the quarterdeck. She knew deep inside her that what she had dreamt was real, that Joe was finally coming home and that it was only a matter of days before he would walk through the door of the cottage.

When she returned from the corner of the room, feeling awkward and stiff in her new silk finery, her father lit the candles and paused as she came into the light, watching her carefully, furtive appreciation deep in his eyes.

Rosie couldn't stand the tension any longer, "Well, what is this all about?" She paused, then risked asking the question, watching his face carefully in the candlelight, "Is Joe coming home?"

His eyes gave her the denial before he could speak, "Joe! That little good-for-nothing! Joe?" He spat on the floor, scowling at her, "No, these little gifts have been provided by my new friends in high places! To keep me sweet and so that I won't start singing songs about their secrets when the music is too low!" He smirked, "They haven't thought about it yet, but I consider that I could get a regular little sum for keeping my mouth shut!" He looked at her sharply, "Forget about Joe! Our new friends will take care of us, you'll see. Joe'll never come home. You'll never see him again. And I don't want to, ever."

Rosie could see him remember the day Joe had left. They stood in silence opposite each other across the deal table, eyes lowered, remembering. Since Joe had left, neither had spoken of it to the other....

Rosie and Joe had been out together all day, high up on the downs, collecting blackberries till the sun sank into the sea. When her father had returned drunk, he had found the cottage empty and had waited for them, drinking steadily. They had returned very late, carrying the two baskets brimming with berries, giggling together softly as they eased the door open quietly, thinking he was asleep. Joe had let Rosie go through the door first, completely unprepared for the heavy hand concealed behind it.

Her father had been waiting behind the door until she was through and had then slammed it shut in Joe's face. Her father's fists rained down on her head and shoulders with a force which shot the basket and the berries over the floor. Rosie had screamed as she fell over, slipping on the berries, unable to get up as he started to kick at her. In her panic, she had been only dimly aware of the door bursting open and Joe hurling himself at the drunken man, crashing his fists into his face. The two had fallen into the red mush on the floor, locked in a vicious fight. Rosie knew that if she didn't do something quickly, one of them would kill the other. She had collected her senses enough to pour cold water over them and they, at last, parted, their breath racking in their chests, each covered from head to knees in dark red congealed juice.

Her father had collapsed on the floor. Joe went to sleep outside. In the morning Joe had gone. She knew where to look for his message and found it stuck in the grating behind the chest at the entrance to Joe's Secret Passage in the ruined cottage above the cliff. He said he was going to sea. He said he would come back for her. He said he loved her. He was the only one who had ever said it.

"I jest gin'en a proper towsin'" Was all her father had to say the next day. And Rosie had waited ever since.

Now, Rosie and her father both kept still, standing opposite each other on each side of the table, each reluctant to break the tension between them. The low growling moan of the gale and the crash of the surf were the only sounds. Rosie looked up at her father, knowing that he knew that she hated him. His eyes in the candlelight looked more yellow than ever, "No, my dear, it's not Joe. It's somebody far more important to us than Joe..."

They only just heard the muffled rap on the door before the latch was pulled down from outside. The door crashed in, the screaming wind pushing in with it a bulk of a man, streaming water from the deluge beyond. Turning slowly, the figure managed to press the door back and finally drew down the latch, grunting and wheezing with the effort. He then turned, removed his sodden bowler hat and bowed low before Rosie. James Wiskard's good eye remained fixed, staring up at her from beneath his bald head as he remained bowed, the other eye examining the table. He slowly stood up, emitting a slow wheeze of appreciation.

For a split second she didn't know if he was looking at the food or at her. Then she realised with a giddy feeling of sickness that his appreciation was directed certainly at her, standing by the table in her fine clothes, softened by the candlelight.

Wiskard glanced quickly up at her father with a look of naked conspiracy. "Tip us out a drop o' wine, matey." He said.

Rosie understood the deal they had struck between them, and why she was standing there in the new fine clothes. Like an animal with no escape, she slid into a chair and put her head in her hands. Her father rushed forward and helped James Wiskard off with his wet overcoat, leaving it steaming on a hook on the back of the door. Both men then sat at the table and uncorked the wine, pouring the three goblets. Wiskard pushed one across the table to Rosie.

She lifted her head but said nothing, staring straight in front of her, unable to look at either of them. Wiskard stood up, his fat calves scraping the chair backwards across the floor, and raised his glass high, "To the Twenty-third day of September in the Year of Our Lord, 1849! And to the wrecking of the Sea Witch, may she give us rich pickings!" he pronounced, holding the goblet up, turning its cut-glass in the light and peering at it as if it were a jewel.

So that was it! The Cornishmen. They were wreckers! Rosie understood it all. The big Cornishman was a professional murderer, expert in the skill of deceiving a captain to take his ship off-course onto the rocks. There had never, ever been a deliberate wrecking on the island, there had never been deliberate murder on the shore. "But... You can't mean.... You can't the sailors, there may be women... there may be children!" Rosie found that she couldn't breathe. She gulped at some of the wine to ease the tightness in her throat.

"Yes, my dear. And now that you understand, you can drink with us to our fortune. You and me shall enjoy the money well, my little bird, you shall have all the finest things of life that my money shall buy." Wiskard smirked down at her, his lips wet with the wine above his thin beard, "We are prepared. The Cornishman is ready. His men are waiting up on the cliff and along the shore." He wheezed in deep satisfaction, looking down at Rosie's father and then turning with an ironic smirk to Rosie, "Let us drink to the skill of the Satan Wrecker! May our fortune hold good! Here, my little mouse, come and nest on my knee." Wiskard suddenly lunged at her, his soft fat hand gripping the blue silk of her dress and pulling her towards him, his lips shiny and coloured with the wine, swollen and puckered in the shape of a kiss. Rosie couldn't fight off his solid weight and strength. Her father rocked back in his chair, laughing as Rosie felt her feet slide across the earth floor towards Wiskard. Frantically, she grasped at the edge of the table but it was no use. One eye fixed on her, bulbous with intent, Wiskard now had two hands round her shoulders, the huge force of his arms pulling her face down to his. Her hair fell in a curtain over his upturned face and the moist pulpiness of his lips above the scratchy beard. She was suffocated by the reek of his wheezing breath in her nose.

She heard the door crash open again. Wiskard's arms suddenly lost their pull and Rosie sprang back from him, sick with nausea, gasping for breath. There, standing huge on the threshhold, lit by the candle against the black night, was the Satan Wrecker himself. Towering in the doorway like an embodiment of the storm he brought in with him, his tarpaulin hat and thick overcoat streamed water in gushing runnels onto the floor, his red hair matted thickly at his flapping collar. In the seconds as both candles guttered in the cold wind, Rosie saw his eyes gleaming green, bright and terrifying as he looked at the group of three round the table.

"Celebrating before the ship arrives, eh, Wiskard?" His ironic voice was still pleasing to the ear, as if trained to draw the listener into a sense of confidence. Rosie knew that to listen to that voice for too long would sap the will completely. Again, he reminded her of a huge predator, "Well, you can give me some of that wine for my men, it'll be some hours yet before we see her lights. Pass me some of those bottles, Cotton!"

As her father lunged for the things on the table in instant obedience, she suddenly recognised the pattern again. The pattern of authority, emanating out of this one man who held complete control. It was only because of this man's power that her father was able to extract money out of the gentry, only because of this one man that the Rector had to speak politely to her father, even at the risk of being seen by others in public. She looked at her father as he fawned, at his sickly smile upturned as he handed over the bottles. She couldn't help her expression showing her contempt for him, but then quickly rearranged her features into the impassive. But looking up, she saw that she was too late - the predator's eyes were on her, assessing her form in the flattering clothes, closely judging the expression which had just left her face.

"Can she be trusted, Cotton?"

"I'll make sure she can be, and so will Wiskard here." muttered her father, drawing in Wiskard as security, "She stands to gain from our good fortune."

"You know that if she can't, I'll have her head and yours! And your bald head too, Wiskard, on a pike! Both of you men be on the cliff within the half-hour!" With that, he turned and marched out of the door, leaving it banging in the hurl of the wind as the spume from the crashing waves splattered across its wooden face.

In the gloom of the dark cottage, Rosie saw Wiskard move across to the wicker basket and carefully put his hand under the white napkins, drawing out two heavy objects which gave a metal clash as they rattled against the silver cutlery inside. He stuck the objects in his belt and drew his jacket tightly across his chest.

"Stay here and don't move till we get back!" Shouted her father as he and Wiskard pulled on their overcoats and edged out of the door into the storm, leaning their shoulders out into the gale and the spray to pull it shut behind them.

Rosie sat in the dark, her knees hunched, for a long time after they left, listening to the vicious deep growl of the gale and the growing fury of the sea as it pounded and hammered the shore, the walls of the cottage and the cliff above her. Her mind was numb, she was caught in a trap, helpless and pathetic. There was nothing she could do. She thought of the men on the ship and knew that they would be killed, if not by the rocks and the sea, then by the merciless killers who waited in the cliffs to butcher anyone who managed to survive the mountainous liquid hills of water as they hurled themselves onto the sharp rocks. Between the maelstrom and those rocks any ship would be ground and torn, she knew, like a wooden box between the rollers of a wringer. There would be no survivors.

Rosie stared up into the rafters as they creaked beneath the thatch, groaning as it took the full brunt of the hammering wind. Before it had been the high scream of a gale-force wind, but now Rosie could hear under the screech a dull growl growing deeper and lower, stronger with malice, she thought. It was the sound of cruelty.

Then she remembered the presence above the rafters in the dark. The one to which she had prayed every night ever since Joe had left. Was it still there even in this storm which was tearing the sky? She desperately needed to reach it, to get through, to get help. She was surrounded by evil, she had to find help.

Rosie got slowly to her feet and put on a thick cloak over her new clothes, tying an old leather belt around her waist to keep her clothes together and taking one of her father's thick caps. At the door, she paused, remembering Wiskard's movements before he left. She went to the wicker basket and dug around under the linen cloth, her fingers recognising the shapes of two pistols. No doubt, her father had meant to take them with him, but had forgotten in his hurry. She quickly stuck them into the folds of her silk dress under the cloak, held firm by the belt. It made her feel better, although she didn't know if the pistols were loaded and only had the vaguest notion of how to use them.

She kicked off the new ladies' shoes and put on her old leather boots. Despite the critical danger, she had time for a wry smile at her appearance. She hoped that the presence in the rafters would overlook her bizarre dress.

But then, she thought, she would have an exclusive audience - the Rector was an evil man and one of the wreckers - there was nobody else for the presence to listen to.

The full force of the wind hit her from the sea as she left the cottage, the waves dark living hills with angry snapping white teeth thumping and clawing at the shingle, huge living beasts in the dark roar of the gale. Breathless, Rosie staggered and stumbled as she was swept up the cliff path and turned towards the road along the top to the old church, already praying, muttering in sobs that were caught and choked in the wind, that the presence in the rafters would be there to meet her.

PART ELEVEN

29

Jane

For four hours I had written out my report to Driscoll. I found an old jiffy bag and a label and put the report inside it. I had only three second-class postage stamps left and hoped it would be enough.

The silence in the bedroom was eerie. The glowing green figures on the old digital clock gave the only light in the bedroom. It was 11.25 p.m. I really did not want to go. Not having slept at all, I was feeling acutely hungry. Despite the low blood sugar, it would be so very easy just to lie down and drift into sleep and wake in the morning, telling myself later that natural fatigue had taken over, that it wasn't my fault that I hadn't got out of bed before much-needed sleep overwhelmed me. The fact is, I didn't want to go. I was frightened.

But I had to. To defer it would risk never having an answer and always to wonder what might have happened.

As my feet touched the floor in the darkened room, I felt that I was formally accepting a challenge. A challenge which came from another time, which only I could take up. I fumbled about, carefully choosing, and very quietly dressing in, the very thickest clothing I could find. Not because it would be cold - simply because I felt more secure and more protected, that the more there was between me and what was about to happen the better - a

223

thick pair of jeans, two dark shirts and a dark-blue jumper, leather baseball boots. I pulled out a thick kapok-lined blue jacket with a high collar. Last, I jerked down tight on my head a green woollen baseball hat, snug with its scratchy thickness, embroidered Philadelphia Eagles (I had bought it on impulse on a trip to New York with my ex, bored and shopping while he did his drug deals). Excited and scared at the same time, I dressed with measured deliberation, queasy and tense, like a gladiator arming for battle.

The landing and stairs were pitch black and I had to feel my way down. At the foot of the stairs I crept through to the kitchen.

Small sounds pricked my imagination, heightened my awareness. I thought of ghosts, of spirits lurking deep in the stone. I quietly searched for a small black vanadium steel pen-torch, checking carefully that its beam was strong. Then I remembered Fiona. What would happen if she woke and found me gone? I scribbled a note and left it on the kitchen table - "Have gone to old church graveyard - back after midnight. If not back by morning......."

As I wrote the words, the skin of my scalp crawled under the tight cap. What could anyone do if I didn't come back? I scrubbed out the last sentence. With care, I turned the key in the lock, went out and gently pulled the front door closed behind me.

I shoved the jiffy bag in the post box, went down from Pier Street past the Winter Gardens to the Quay and then turned left along the mile of concrete embankment to Bonchurch and Monks Bay. Outside in the blackness the moonlight defined the empty path in harsh white. The bubbling sound of the surf sounded close and clear in the dark.

At Monks Bay I climbed the path. The occasional hiss of leaves and clicky chatter of grasshoppers were the only other sounds. The track looked narrower than it did in daylight, the tall sycamores at the cliff-edge reaching out at me over the black shadows under their branches, stems of bushes and brambles reached out and touched my hair and shoulders as I passed, as if in farewell. I climbed through the hole in the wall to the cliff path. A startling rustle of bushes. There was a cat at my feet! I stood still for a moment, breathing slowly and deeply, calming myself. The cat rubbed against my leg. Both of us, the cat and I, were grateful for the unexpected company, to find another living creature in the still, dark world frozen by the full moon.

I began walking the path along the cliff edge. To one side, waves crept softly into the beach under the cliff, unfolding in thin flourescent bars, growing in length behind and ahead of me. On the other side, tortured silhouettes of trees showed black like sentinels on the hill against the cold stars. I brushed between rows of milk-white yarrow flowers. The moonlight reflected on the sea kept slow pace, marking my progress. The yarrow scent was like incense.

I stopped halfway along the cliff, staring out to sea, looking at the thin waves, the only moving things in the vast still night under the moon and stars. I finally had to admit to myself that I was terrified. But then, after I accepted it, fear sank into a corner of my mind, leaving space for me to think more clearly. The grasses rustled. A single bedroom light glowed yellow in East Dene Manor and then went out.

I looked at my watch. It was exactly ten minutes before midnight as I descended into the blackness at the end of the path. The sound of the sea receded suddenly. A sweet damp odour of green filled the stillness. Nettles and brambles caught at my legs. I nervously felt for the torch, switched it on and twisted it to concentrate the beam.

At the corner where the church stood, a strong gust jerked the branches into life, as if the trees were startled by my unexpected arrival from the cliff. I stopped at the wall. The iron gate to the graveyard was half-open - half inviting, half declining my entrance. "The choice is yours", it said. A dense black tree crouched just inside the gate, overhanging, waiting for my decision.

I kept the torch on as I went in.

30

The flint path was stark in the full moon, winding through the tombs towards the porch. Creeping past the larger headstones near the entrance, my imagination saw the bones inside them, the eye-sockets in the skulls peering at me from inside the stone boxes. Hesitantly, I ran the torchlight along the deep green darkness under the bushes, startled as shapes of gravestones leapt up in the beam, each one a different stone character, a different shape, caught in the sudden light like conspirators, robbers in stealthy ambush or like dark monks brooding on private sins, before the light passed on and they shrank silently back to the shadows. A narrow path ran down into the hollow. Two huge fir trees stood darkly over the church, branches splayed out wide against the starlight, as if poised to bend in silent greeting. The gravestones resembled a waiting crowd, curved heads and square thin bodies, at all angles. Some in close pairs, some in intimate groups, some standing aloof from the others, like the forms of the dead under their feet. A close sudden rustle of leaves only deepened the silence. As I descended the steep path between the stones, I felt their gaze upon my back as I passed by, waiting until I was in the centre of them, at the bottom of the hollow, before they moved at me. I trod carefully, keeping my feet away from the soil at the edge of the narrow path, aware of the dead under the ground. "Only six feet under," I remembered the phrase, glad of the thick soles on my shoes.

Reaching the bottom, I quickly turned to look back up the path. The path looked thinner now, almost lost in the thick waiting crowd pressing down above me. They stood absolutely still, but I was sure that the stones had closed in behind me in the darkness of the slope. To escape at all, to get back to the gate, I would have to pass through their midst. It was easier to go on.

It seemed that I was the only living thing left, being watched with cold indifference by the trees and the stones as I delicately picked my way towards the far corner nearest the sea.

Then, as I approached the big stone plinth, I heard a noise.

But it was nothing more than the sound of the water from the spring as it bubbled along by the edge of the graveyard towards the cliff edge. Then, listening to it, I realised that I could also hear in the very distance the slow rustle of the surf on the shore. With a last glance over my shoulder at the waiting crowd of gravestones, mentally bidding them goodbye, I squeezed through the small space at the very corner of the graveyard and then, with a mounting sense of occasion, checking over my shoulders to the right and left, I finally brought myself to stand in the very centre of the small clear space between the graves and the plinth. I switched off the torch and put it in my jacket pocket. I stood up straight, legs apart, and for some reason put my hands together behind my back. Then I raised my eyes to look straight up at the face of the figurehead, bright and clear in the moonlight.

But nothing happened. The face was still scarred and damaged, the features flat. The wood was still rotten.

I kept my head up for a long time, examining every mark on the face, every grain of the rotten wood, until my eyes ached, trying to see some sign of life in the remains of the impassive face. Still nothing happened. Still there was silence in the small space. Only the brook babbling, only the distant slish-slush of the gentle surf.

I closed my eyes. I was a complete idiot! Who else would be standing here in a corner of a graveyard at midnight looking up at the face of a rotten figurehead? With a surge of relief, I suddenly laughed out loud at my stupid gullibility. The whole thing was ridiculous - a stupid illusion. How could I let myself be carried away? The stones were just stones. Those idiots, the Spiritualists, they were raving lunatics. My imagination had got the better of me yet again. Maybe it was low blood sugar, lack of sleep, worry. Maybe I was going mad. I thrust my hands deep into the comfort of my pockets and pulled my collar up. I glanced round the space again. Poor fools, I thought. Poor fools. All of them and their silly voices.

Angrily I shouldered past the stone plinth. The Time! What a fool I had been. The Cycle! What a joke. Hocus Pocus! I walked quickly across the dell and climbed up the path between the gravestones, not caring if I trod on the graves or not. The dead were dead. They didn't have spirits. Just rotten bones. As I climbed, I kicked out angrily at the gravestones to prove the point. "There is no magic!" I muttered, "There are no spirits! There is nothing! There is nothing!"

"*Nothing unless you find it in yourself.*"

I stopped, flinching. It was the Voice. Unmistakeable. The same voice. My feet were pinned, unable to move. I couldn't lift my eyes to look at what I had just seen at the very edge of my vision, the terror of it pumping over me in waves of sweat. There was something at the top of the path, waiting for me. I jerked my eyes up. There it was, towering above me, tall and erect with commanding power, completely still at the top of the path. Her gown fell to her feet like a vast column framed in the dark arch of the porch. Her hands glowed white at each side, as if carved out of the long gown. Thick black hair cascaded back and fell down to her shoulders, each side of her upturned face, shimmering with white fire in the moonlight. The Sea Witch. The Witch had come.

First I thought her eyes were closed. But then I saw her eyes looking down at me over sharp cheekbones, smiling down at me. She spoke again, "Are you cold, Jane?"

Her voice was beautiful, a cool clear melody, the meaning of the words moving the still air. "I will warm you." The tones in her voice brought warmth and I felt a glow pervade my whole body, a feeling of wonderful comfort and ease. Fear had gone. I looked up at her face, beautiful in the moonlight, an aura of supreme grace and gentleness, her statuesque figure clothed in long white robes, her eyes radiating warmth and kindness as she looked down at me, a smile perfectly formed. I felt myself sliding, slipping into her warmth, into a trance. "I am entranced," I thought, dreamily realising that the word also meant that she had entered into me. I didn't mind. I felt joyful. Full of a wonderful sweet bliss, of a calm enchantment which I had never felt before. I gazed at her in rapture, taken over by a complete submission to her will, basking in her light, in captivation. "I am captivated," The thought floated about like coloured mist in my mind, captured in the warm cell of thoughts, "I am captured"

The words wriggled free from the warm haze in my brain and sat there waiting for me in the front of my mind. "I am a prisoner!" The words said, "I am a prisoner!" More of my mind escaped from the warm haze. Suddenly all of my mind had escaped and I could see the words clearly, "I am a prisoner!"

"I am not a prisoner!" I muttered. I looked up at the Witch. Was it imagination, or had her expression changed? The expression in her eyes was changing, I was sure. The smile had gone.

"What is your purpose, Jane?" The voice had changed too, there was an edge to it, a sharp edge. The beautiful woman had disappeared, each of her features developing into something horrible. I could see the original forms still in the hunched little hag who now stood in the porch, her long filthy nails scratching at the wooden door as she seethed, each of her features had shown their other side, painted by a crazed lunatic. This revolting creature now turned in a fury, "You little fool!"

Spittle seeped between her rotten teeth, "They destroyed me - my husband, my son." The bitter screech of her laughter rang out across the graves. She coughed, her withered fingers pulling at the thin bloodless lips, her sunken eyes staring out wildly at me from dark sockets, "You little fool! You fool!" The dark ragged figure bit into her wrist, wracked by hate, "You shame me. You think it's a game? Selling your cheap silly little mind-games? Which you do not yourself believe in?"

Her eyes glared up at me from above the sleeve and she pulled her mouth out of it to spit the words, her voice deep and gasping with the memory, with the need for spiteful revenge, "And now the Time has indeed come, the Cycle is full turned at last! The fifteen decades has come and gone at last."

Cold seeped into the pit of my stomach, my weight pulling me down. I knelt on the ground, eyes closed, back against a gravestone. The Witch looked down at me impatiently, then paused, "All men have a capacity for evil. But so do we."

I looked up at her, again surprised. Her tone had changed, this time fuller, more rounded, more kind, a gentle sadness in her voice, a smile of regret on her finely shaped lips. "I am elemental, earth, fire, air and water. I am the Moon Goddess. The Blue Dragon." She looked down at me, her sneer guttural and raw, "I need to wipe the slate clean."

Stiffly, I pushed myself up off the ground and staggered after her as she turned and glided back into the porch. Inside, the ancient wooden door opened before her of its own accord as she entered the darkness of the church. Inside, the moonlight shone in a broad, bright beam from the main chancel window behind the altar cross. I followed the Witch between the pews to the altar and stood beside her, facing towards the sea. She was still the beautiful, radiant woman of moments before and now she looked down at me kindly as we stood either side of the cross. "Look through the window."

I gazed out at the moonlit sea, at the bar of reflected light which spread across the surface of the water towards me, like an avenue of silver light reaching to the horizon, "I can only see the sea and the moon, nothing else." I murmured.

"Look carefully, my dear, look carefully at the very rim of the sea under the moon. What do you see there, Jane?" Her voice sounded calm, murmuring softly in the stillness.

"There's a bright spot, directly under the moon, the brightest spot, at the top of the silver avenue... Like a crescent..."

"Look at it hard and long, hard and long. Study it carefully, keep looking 'til your eyes ache..."

I kept my eyes open, not blinking, looking hard. Watching the bright spot, it seemed to get brighter. I kept looking.

"Now close your eyes," Her voice grew softer, "... and tell me what you see..."

I shut my eyes, concentrating on the shapes which I could see against the darkness of my eyelids, "I can see the same shape, only it's yellow.... no, now it's black.... but it's still the same shape.... like a bowl... very clear..."

"Yes. Draw the bowl towards you, draw it closer, towards you..." Her voice had now become very soft, almost as if it was now inside my head, as if she was standing with me inside my head, watching the dark shape of the bowl moving towards us.

"Can you see how big and close it is? So close, it's almost touching your feet, so big you could almost step into it?" Her voice became distant, as if it was fading away. She was no longer standing with me. I was alone, watching the big bowl at my feet.

Disembodied, her soft voice whispered soothingly in my mind, "Step into the bowl, step into the bowl at your feet....," I felt my feet move and, against my closed eyelids, watched my foot fall forward into the dish. As I fell forward, I thought I heard the Witch behind and above me, her voice still soft.

"Where am I going?" I murmured.

"Into the moondish," I heard her reply, "You are going to see for yourself...."

It was the word which woke me up. That strange word, "the moondish". I opened my eyes with a start. It was still dark and the Witch had disappeared. Looking up from where I lay stretched out on the floor, there was no moonlight. The cross had gone too. The howl of a raging storm outside reverberated throughout the length of the building.

I got to my feet and looked around. Even in the gloom, I could see that the inside of the church had changed. The chancel window was a different shape, much smaller, and instead of the ornate stonework, there was only bare plaster. The place smelt strongly of damp and neglect. In rising panic, I looked back down the length of the nave. The pews had changed! They had sides waist-high with little panelled doors. There was a wooden gallery at the east end. I lurched forward down the nave, looking for the door in the darkness. Fumbling, I took out my pen-torch and switched it on.

Then I saw her.

In the back of the small vestibule, her blue silk gown and pearl necklace shining in the torch-light, crouched a girl, looking up at me, eyes wide with fright under thick chestnut hair which fell over her face as she trembled. She was so terrified that her open mouth formed the shape of a scream but only a thin sound emerged. She was pointing a gun at me - an old gun - a sort of flintlock pistol.

"It's alright, it's alright!" I shouted against the storm outside. "I'm a friend! Look!" I pointed the torch up in my face, showing the green baseball hat. Slowly, she shut her mouth and looked at me in dumbfounded amazement. Trying to get her voice back with a swallow, she looked at me again, frowning slightly, trying to grapple with a difficult, an inconceivable idea. Then she had the answer. She looked up at me standing in front of her in the middle of the church, forming a question, but looking certain that she already knew the answer. "You've come from the rafters?" She asked breathlessly, "You've come to help me."

31

I kept the torch on her as she got to her feet. Her muddy leather boots and crumpled cap, the pearls and shining blue folds of her dress making her seem terribly fragile, terribly beautiful, like a princess having been dragged through mud by rough soldiers from the steps of a grand ball. She walked slowly towards me, hand outstretched, still pointing the pistol. "I cannot see your face behind the lantern, please show me your face. Again." Even against the bluster and groan of the wind, I was struck by her voice, rich and low with a strong accent. It was lovely. "What is your name?"

"Jane. Can you put that pistol away, please?" By comparison, I am sure that my voice sounded high and squeaky in the damp space. "My name is Jane Tench."

She looked at me, squinting in the glare of the torch, frowning, "But Jane Tench is mad. Everyone knows. She's to be taken away." Then, "Show your face."

I pointed the thin beam of the torch straight at my own face, lighting it up clearly under the peak of my cap, squinting in the glare. She recoiled as I did it, raising the pistol again. "But you're so young!"

I saw her decide to trust me. As she reached forward and clutched my arm, her eyes in the light were beautiful.

"My name is Rosie, Rosie Cotton."

I grasped her arm. "What's the date today?"

"It's September..." Rosie remembered Wiskard saying it as he had raised his glass, ".. .the twenty-third day of September..."

"But the year, what's the year?"

"In the Year of Our Lord Eighteen Hundred and Forty-Nine."

I stepped across to the wall and ran my hand along the damp plaster, the dim shapes of a fresco mixed in with stains. It was solid. The animal howl of the wind outside was real. "She's sent me back! To see for myself." I muttered idiotically, trying to think clearly, "The wrecking!"

"So you know of it? You know of the wrecking?" Rosie was pulling me towards the door.

"Yes, I know all about the wrecking!" Oddly, neither of us thought this at all strange. In the apex of acute tension this strange remark passed by both of us as a mere detail.

"We must get help! We'll go to Mister Dickens!" She pulled me through the church porch and out into the wind. Even in the dark, I could see that there were fewer gravestones. It was easy to run between them as Rosie led me up to the back wall, easy to climb over and drop into the garden of Winterbourne house. All the lights were out. I mean, of course, that no candles shone in the windows. The climbing rose on the verandah shook in the gusting wind as we reached its shelter.

"He's got to be in here" Rosie peered through the glass door of the french windows and turned the handle. We went in. Closing the glass door behind us, in the sudden stillness inside the solid house, I switched the torch on again. We crept between armchairs with lace macassars and small tables to a big double door at the rear. Beyond it, wincing at the small squeak of the hinges, we saw a staircase and quickly ran up the thickly carpeted stairs. On the landing, several doors gave into bedrooms, some open, some closed. We tried the first one to the south. Inside, there was a huge desk underneath a large window looking over the garden and the sea. The desk was neatly clear, except for a small pile of papers at one side. I approached it, fascinated. The desk of Charles Dickens himself. I pulled at some of the papers, glancing at them in the light of the torch, reading the lines of elegant, neatly florid handwriting. Rosie came over, pulling at my arm. "Look at this!" I said.

Despite her anxiety, she obeyed, and we both bent over the handwriting as I drew the small beam across the lines, whispering the words quickly as I read them..."*The room was a pleasant one, at the top of the house, overlooking the sea, on which the moon was shining brilliantly. After I had said my prayers and the candle had burnt out, I remember how I still sat looking at the moonlight on the water, as if I could hope to read my fortune in it, as in a bright book; or to see my mother with her child, coming from Heaven, along that shining path, to look upon me as she had looked when I last saw her sweet face. I remember how the solemn feeling with which at length I turned my eyes away, yielded to the sensation of gratitude and rest which the sight of the white-curtained bed ...*"

"Come on, We've got to find him and wake him up!" I shook her off, and carried on reading the words. "*..... I remember how I thought of all the solitary places under the night sky where I had slept, and how I prayed that I never* *might be houseless any more, and never might forget the houseless. I remember how I seemed to float, then, down the melancholy glory of that track upon the sea, away into the world of dreams."*

The last sentence had an eerie familiarity. "My God!" I said, "He's describing the moondish, that's what happened to me! Down the track into a world of dreams."

"But this, t'is not a world of dreams," Whispered Rosie, grabbing my arm and shaking me. "This is real and so is that ship which is coming and so are those wreckers! Now come on!"

As we turned, we saw a small figure in the doorway looking at us. A very small boy with thin shoulder-length hair and a big round head. "Who are you?" He asked, rubbing his eyes.

"We seek your papa," whispered Rosie urgently, "Can you show us where he sleeps, please?" She moved towards the little boy, "What is your name, my little one?"

"Sidney Smith Haldimand Dickens." The boy recited his name automatically, "And papa is not here. He is magnetising John Leech who is very ill. At Hill Cottage. He got hit by a wave." Said the small boy. Then, as an afterthought, as sleep began to return, "Do you want to speak to mama?"

"No thank you, Sidney, you may go back to sleep now."

The little boy simply turned and left the room. "Now will you come on, Jane?"

As we reached the door to the garden, Rosie pulled the door open and whispered, "Dout the light! Put out the lantern, it's too dangerous! They're all over the cliff above the shoal."

I obeyed, pulling my collar up and my cap down, leaning against the wind and rain outside. A streak of lightning angled and cracked between the clouds. There were many more trees than I remembered, now all writhing and torn in the blackness. Rosie led me down the track, a much longer track than I remembered. Instead of a cliff path the track was wide, hard and smooth, made of flint, but the sky was so black, I could barely see where we were treading. Rosie stopped me in the lee of a wall, pointing out to sea. I made to speak, but she pressed her hand over my mouth, drawing back a clutch of hair, offering her ear to my mouth. I felt very close to her as I spoke, remembering the spidery writing in the ship's log, *"Watch for a distress flare. And blue lights...."*

Just as I said it, a flare shot up from along the coast, curving yellow in the sky then suddenly dipping sharply into the sea, blown down hard by the wind. I stared out to sea, knowing that even as I watched, Adam's great-great-grandfather was writing the final entry in the log of the Sea Witch, that his hand had just laid the pen to rest in his cabin as he ordered the firing of the rockets and the lighting of the blue lights as the great ship drew in on the final beat to its death on the rocks....

Eyes narrowed and watering, we peered into the very teeth of the gale, shivering, holding onto each other. The orange rockets shot up from far out on the water, hurling high into the sky, carried in on the gusting wind to smash into the side of the cliff. Rosie suddenly tugged at my coat, pressing her lips against my ear, "The blue lights!" I squinted out to where she pointed. Then I saw the slight form of the ship and her square sails, dwarfed and rolling under the huge Atlantic swell, grey mountains of water in the black night. The Sea Witch was coming in, tiny blue specks of light in her lower rigging.

Rosie pressed her lips to my ear again. "The shoal! We must get to the shoal," She yelled, tugging at my coat.

We ran and stumbled as fast as we could along the road. I saw with surprise that it turned down towards the beach and I could just make out the small dark shape of the Boathouse under the foot of the cliff. It had a different roof, it was made of thick thatch, the slate tiles gone. I barely recognised the cliff top below Luke's cottage - the sycamores had gone, the outline more bare, more stark than I remembered. Then I had an idea, "Let's get some rope! Some rope!" I yelled into Rosie's face, pointing down at the Boathouse. She looked at me, hesitated, and then nodded. We rushed down the road and reached the crashing maelstrom on the shore, barely able to stand up against the force of the screaming gale, rain and spume being blown in from the sea in hard straight horizontal lines like bullets.

"The latch! Help me with the latch" I wrenched at it with my whole strength, ramming it up with the palm of my hand. It suddenly gave way and we fell together into the inside of the cottage, stumbling, falling to the floor. Winded, awkwardly, I got to my feet and put my back to the door, feet slipping as I pressed backward to shut it with a crash.

Rosie had fallen backwards and lay on the floor gasping, "What is the matter?" She looked up at my face which felt ashen white, staring into the cottage, towards the single candle burning on the table.

She turned and screamed. There was a man sitting at the table, drinking, one eye looking at me. It could only be. It was Wiskard. He was pointing a pistol straight at my chest as I leant back against the door. He was frowning.

Suddenly it was very quiet inside the closed space. Since he had the gun, I waited, trying to figure out which of his eyes was looking at me. Then I saw both eyes swivel up to look at my hat. He took another sip of wine, keeping the pistol steady, pointing at the middle of my stomach. His frown deepened.

"And what, pray, are the Philadelphia Eagles?" He enquired politely, almost lazily.

We gazed at him blankly. Then Rosie looked up from the floor. Her gaze slowly lifted to my green baseball hat. "Philadelphia Eagles!" She read out slowly, stumbling over the pronunciation of the first word.

"It's a baseball team. American. Twentieth century....they're very good." I finished lamely, watching the end of the pistol barrel pointing at my guts.

Wiskard smiled to himself, "I really must give up this drinking," He said, musing, "I will become teetotal, it's a promise. After we get the silver...." He suddenly sprang to his feet and grabbed Rosie by the hair, bending her head back, "Now! Enough of this idiocy! Where did you find this lunatic and who is she?"

"She's from the rafters," Rosie choked as she tried to get the words out.

"The rafters? What do you mean, you little slut?" Wiskard wrenched her head back with savage force on each syllable of his words, "The rafters. The rafters?" He yelled. "If you do not cease this nonsense forthwith, I'll shoot her now and have done with it!" He raised the pistol to my head. I closed my eyes. "Damn the Sea Witch!" I thought.

"Sea Witch?" Wiskard was looking at me carefully with one of his eyes. I hadn't been aware that I had said the words. "What do you know about the Sea Witch?"

I had an inspiration. It was a risk I would have to follow through with, but I didn't have any choice. I pushed my weight off the door and stood up straight, With an intake of breath I lunged forward and grabbed the pistol from Wiskard's grip, thankful it hadn't exploded in my hand.

"Well, well!" Both Wiskard's eyes were fixed on me. His voice grew smooth, "You see Missy, I hate violence... as I am sure that you do... It'll all be over soon, so why don't you just put away that pistol? Eh?"

Rosie scuttled into the recesses of the cottage and came back with two lengths of rope, neatly tied.

"Who are you?" Wiskard growled at me, "Who are you?"

"Tie him up!" I kept the gun pointed at Wiskard's head, trying to decide whether all I needed to do was just pull the trigger or whether I had to cock or prime something beforehand to make it work.

Rosie did so, with the quick efficiency of a fisherman's daughter. I made to check the knots, acutely aware that I knew nothing about them at all, "You're certain they're O.K.?"

"O.K.? What does that mean? I am sure they won't be undone, if that is what you intend to say." She looked at me strangely. I blew out the candle and we left Wiskard in the dark as I shut the door hard, checking that the latch was firmly down.

32

Monks Bay. Isle of Wight. 23rd September, 1849.

Out on the shore, I felt tiny - a mere insect at the feet of forces as old and hard as obsidian. The huge cliffs, the mountains of waves, the deep venom and scream of the wind - how could I really have thought that I could do anything? I clutched at the rope, fingering its roughness, trying to give myself some courage. People were about to die, crushed and twisted, flung by the sea and smashed on the rocks, their humanity lost, reduced to nothing - torn skin and broken bones to be left floating and then finally to sink in the cold indifference of the sea.

Even the thick padding of my jacket couldn't withstand the freezing fingers of wind creeping up my back. Rosie pulled at my arm, "Come on! Come on!" She peered carefully at my face, seeing my thoughts. "Come on! If we aren't there we can do nothing. There's still a chance!"

I staggered after her along the thin beach, tripping over rocks, every movement an effort. It didn't take long for us to reach the shoal. As Rosie led me, creeping in behind some large rocks at the foot of the cliff, I remembered how Luke had done the same thing. I sat in sudden misery. How was I going to get back? Would I be able to at all, or was I stuck forever in this violent world? Rosie was pulling at my coat again, pointing upwards, jerking her finger up at the cliff. Up there on a slight mound I saw the spout lantern flash again, believing I could see a group of dark figures each side, grey against the black face of the cliff. The rolling mountains of water relentlessly pounded at the foot of the cliff, the next climbing on top of its predecessor, higher and higher, pushed forward by the angry swell of the ones behind. Sharp lightning cracked. One explosion built on the other until the whole sky was lit up in cold blue. In the clear light I could see the figures up on the cliff. And now I could see the ship. It was close in.

One mast had already gone, dragging across the deck. On a lee shore, the nightmare of every sailor, the ship was totally at the mercy of the wind and sea driving it into the surf like a bird with broken wings. The lightning died for a moment and then arched across the whole sky, one crack after another, making it easy to see the tiny figures strewn across the deck as the whole ship suddenly rose up on the mighty shoulders of a great wave, lurching forward, bow driving straight at the foot of the cliff, the length of its bowsprit pointing upward like a lance.

Then something happened. The lightning came out from behind the clouds and filled the sky with stark white light. It didn't crash or flicker. It just stayed there, filling the scene with burning clarity. Even the wave seemed to stall before the base of the cliff, carrying the ship on its shoulders, rearing up at something above it. I clutched hold of Rosie. Then I looked up and understood. High above us on a spur of the cliff, there stood the big man. He stood alone, legs apart, like a rock, looking down straight at the front of the ship as it reared up at him. He gripped the spout lantern with both hands and pointed it down at the ship. Even in that moment of startling clarity, the beam from the spout-lantern seemed to pick out the proud figurehead, the yellow light making the white lady under the lance of the bowsprit come alive as she looked up at the man on the cliff. There were only the two of them. The betrayed looked up at the betrayer. Time had stopped.

I felt Rosie's hand slide under my jacket and grip round me tight as she turned her head away, pushing it deep against my shoulder. As I looked back, I saw the ship begin to move again. It reared high, higher still on the great wave until the white lady was on the same level as the man on the cliff, still straining upward. I could feel every timber of the ship grinding under strain, every line of her fragile frame tortured as she rose.

Then the lightning died and went out. In the black, I heard the fall of the wave and a noise beneath the wind which made my blood congeal. It was the noise of a long groaning crash, like a solid wooden box splitting under the slow weight of a steamroller, deafening as the keel of the ship ground and splintered, forced across the rocks by the force of the water, right up onto the shore.

In the seething white of the surf, I could see clearly the black front of the ship, like a wall suddenly stuck in the sand and pebbles. The bow-sprit had broken off and the figurehead had gone. Now I could hear screams. I saw men scrambling over the sides, their dark shapes fall into the water and then stand in the surf, groping towards the shore, crawling forward right to the edge of the beach and then suddenly, for no reason, just when they had reached the point of safety, falling over as if giving up hope, drawn back into the clutch and suck of the undertow.

I moved forward, tugging the rope undone, but Rosie pulled me back with all her strength. "You'll be killed!"

Annoyed she should suddenly change our plan I roughly tried to shake her off but she got her hands round my head and we fell onto the sand struggling. To my amazement, she sank her teeth into my ear, the sharp pain mixing with her words as she held onto me, gasping, "You fool! They'll shoot you! They're shooting them in the water! Like dogs as they reach the land!"

I stopped and listened. With a sick feeling, I then understood why they were giving up hope. I heard the little sharp sounds under everything else. The sound of guns. The wreckers were waiting on the shore, waiting until the poor seamen had struggled to the sand, within close range, clear dark shapes against the white surf, and then shot them.

I pushed myself up, pulling at the long rope. "Rosie, help me," I screamed at her, "Tie it round my waist! Hold onto one end and let it out as I go into the water!" I helped her bend the rope twice round my chest and waited while she fumbled her numb fingers with the stiff rope. Beyond the spray, I could still see a group of figures at the stern of the ship. I started to shove myself out between the rocks, against the waves, into the crash of the freezing water. I pushed against the rocks and hauled myself out into the swell, teeth chattering, choking on the brine as the salt stung in my mouth and nostrils. I pushed on, looking over to the stern of the ship. There were still two figures there, cowering under the lee of the gunwhale, white hair of one showing over the rim. Towards the prow, another two held each other, a man and a young woman. I looked at the water between us. It was too rough. I would never make it, especially with the weight and drag of the heavy rope. I could make out great timbers floating in the sea as the waves hit at the side of the ship, splintering its sides. Unless I could float on one of those timbers and kick through the water, I would never be able to make it across the gap. I looked back at Rosie, a small dim figure back behind the rocks, still clutching onto the other end of the rope. Then something hit me hard in the back, knocking me over. For a moment, I thought I had been shot. But I managed to get my head back above water and I could still move my arms and legs without pain. Then I saw what had hit me. A large white shape floated in the surf, knocking at the rocks. It was the figurehead! She waited there, heavy wood, floating like a boat. The means to rescue the men! Without thinking, I leapt out at the figurehead, gripping numb fingers onto the carved woodwork and started to kick out with my legs, pointing the head towards the stern of the ship. Slowly, slowly, the weight of the figurehead moved out over the surging mounds of water into the deep swell. Then, it was suddenly easier. The tide must have turned. Despite the wind, I was being drawn out to sea. All I had to do was kick to steer, bringing the figurehead in under the high stern. I looked up. Eyes streaming with stinging salt water, I saw four faces, saw the three men helping the girl, saw them grip the rigging, emerge over the rim of the gunwhale, ready to leap. As their bodies hit the water they clung on to the raft of the ship's figurehead. Two older men, the poor girl and then the other one - young, light-coloured hair like wet silk across his forehead.

The older men grabbed the rope and looped it over the wooden head and we all kicked out as we pointed the head and rode the figurehead towards the shore.

Rosie must have seen us, because I could feel a rhythmic tugging as the figurehead was pulled in, aided by our kicking as we floated. She came down the beach as we got to the rocks and staggered over to us as I helped the girl in the dark towards her. She had wound the rope around a big rock and had pulled it in as we came in, easing our passage through the water. Now, she leant out and helped the older men ashore. I gripped the arm of the young man and took his weight as he leant on my shoulder. Without a word we followed Rosie along the beach, numb and dripping with freezing water. The young man staggered and fell against me and I had to keep him up as we stumbled along after Rosie. I didn't know where she was taking us and was too exhausted to care. I dimly knew that we were climbing a small track up to the top of the cliff. As we climbed, I heard a new sound under the wind and the water. A crazy clanging symphony, dreadful to the ear, a juddering discord of the music of death like the sound of twenty pianos being hurled and splintered on the rocks. I looked back. The keel had broken. A great ragged hole had opened up where the spine of the ship had broken. Black shapes, tea-chests, spewed into the surf. Men on ropes splashed into the opening. When we finally reached the top, I was amazed to find myself staring directly at Luke's cottage. Then I became aware of lights below us, loud voices following us right up the path. The wreckers! They must have found the rope on the beach. In panic, I stumbled ahead to Rosie. "They're coming up the path behind us!" I yelled into her face. To my surprise, she just nodded and pointed to Luke's house and I went back to help the fair-headed man to his feet as again we stumbled up the track as fast as we could.

Luke's house was old and derelict. Rosie pulled open the rotting door, nearly falling off its hinges, and closed it behind us as we fell into the darkness inside. She led us down some stairs into the cellar. Then she paused in the pitch blackness. I heard her pulling at something, something which scraped across the stone floor. Then the clank of iron. "Quickly! All of you, in here!"

Rosie looked at me, "Your lantern?" I felt in my pocket and took out the torch, twisting the end of it, praying that the salt water hadn't got inside it. It worked! I shone the light, first at the older man, then at the crumpled form of the young one, then at Rosie.

"Where's the Doctor? Where's Miss Capper?" The old man tried to stand, "Joe? Joe, go find 'em, quick now."

Rosie's eyes stared in disbelief, her mouth open, unable to speak, just like she had stared at me in the church.

"Rosie! What's the matter?" I kept the torch on her face. Still she didn't speak. She was crying. She pointed at the young man, her arm shaking as she tried to say something, trembling uncontrollably as she leant back against the wall. I shone the torch back on him as he lay on the ground. There was a glinting ooze of blood in the torchlight, dark red all across the damp cloth of his shirt. He had been shot! No wonder he had staggered and fallen on the cliff path.

In shock, I looked back at Rosie. Her face had gone white as titanium zinc in the glare of the torch. I went to her and held her up against the wall, the other man supporting her other side. "Rosie! Rosie! There's nothing we can do. We'll have to get him into the tunnel, try to stand up!" I tried to keep the torch on her face as she looked up at me. Then I saw something in her expression which terrified me. She didn't look like Rosie any more. Something had happened beyond the shock and fatigue. Something had gone from inside her. She closed her eyes and leant her head against mine, her whisper clear to us all as she looked down at the boy at her feet. "It's Joe." She said, her whole body shaking against mine, "My brother Joe." Then she collapsed in my arms.

We dragged Joe's body into the tunnel and drew the iron grill across the passage, pulling the old wooden chest back from within. Between us, me leading, gripping the thin torch between my teeth, we carried Rosie along until we were deep inside. I took off my wet jacket and laid Rosie's head on it, hoping that she wouldn't catch a chill. At least it was soft, I thought. I didn't know what to do. She could only sleep and I hoped that sleep would be enough for the moment, but I knew deep down that nothing would be enough now. Something had died in her. I had seen it. I had seen it in her face.

Then, when I heard their dragging footsteps, I knew that nothing could save us. The yellow glow of a lantern showed up in the tunnel outside the door of the chamber where we all cowered. We were like rats. There was no escape. I was amazed that it took so long for the men to arrive. I could hear a scraping and pushing then a pause and then more scraping and pushing. There were no voices. The light got slowly stronger. The old men sat in silence, shivering in their cold, wet clothes, waiting for the end. At last, the edge of a big chest appeared in the glow of light at the door and a face peered over it, startled, staring at us in the chamber. A big head, wet red hair.

I felt close to collapse with exhaustion, weak and numb. My mind was closing over, my fatigue and the cold beginning to draw sleep over my eyes like a thick blanket. I couldn't fight it.

"Don't move. Who's the dead one down the passage?"

"My brother."

I was too tired even to turn my head to look at Rosie. I only remember feeling relieved that she had woken up. I heard her move into a sitting position, "You've broken my heart."

I was staggered at the calm certainty in her voice. But there was something else there too, a deathly fatigue - all the life and hope had gone out of it. And into the emptiness had come a sound which I had never heard before in any living voice. A cold strength of will had formed and was carried out in her words to the man as she spoke next. A tangible force of will which came from Rosie's soul. "I will kill you." She whispered.

The force of her words made the big man step back. In his eyes, I saw a silent acknowledgement and an understanding as he bent his head low over his chest. He didn't flinch or bother to make way as a younger face appeared by his shoulder, a face of a young god, handsome, wet dark hair emphasising the elegant forehead. "Rosie! In the name of the Lord God! How?"

"Nathan." The will in Rosie's voice was fleetingly touched by sadness, but returned instantly with all its strength. "In the name of the Lord, Nathan, you are going to die."

"And I will carry it out."

A choking voice from the door. A dim shape, black clothes running with water, a ghastly face, livid scars, drenched and matted hair. The face of the figurehead which had saved us, made human.

"Alice! My God, No!"

His teeth started to chatter and he started to babble, his eyes staring and bulging in the glow of the lamp, fingers pulling frantically at his earlobe. "It's not my fault, it's not my fault. Alice, Rosie, it was for the good of everyone. I told you what it was like, my father, the government. Please Rosie, you must understand. Yes! Yes, I regret. Yes! I am truly sorry but.... but it's not my fault. I am a social experiment. I am an agent for great change. I see things differently from the rest, *I'm different from other people.*" Nathan began to giggle. Wave after wave of shrieking giggles tugged him down to his knees. But as I looked, I saw that his eyes had filled with tears and that as he knelt the giggles changed to helpless sobbing, "It is a good cause, Rosie, a good cause....Alice, please."

As I listened, my eyes dropped to the lantern on the floor, gazing into the heart of the flame, shining bright behind the glass, magnified by semi-circular lens in its brass cover. I still couldn't move. I couldn't even lift my head up to turn to look at Rosie. My brain had lost its connection with my limbs. I just stared at the flame, the orange glow in the lantern, warming my mind. When I closed my eyes, the dark shape of the lens echoed black against my eyelids. I started to re-live with dreamlike horror all that had happened on the shore. But when I had heard Alice speak to him, when I saw him lower his head, I understood then that I had heard that voice once before and only once before. In the voice of the Sea Witch. It was the sound of the seared core, the voice of the betrayed female soul.

Voices came and went in the blackness. I seemed to hear Rosie's voice again and then Nathan's voice, young and refined, his gabbling finished, shout out suddenly, crystal clear, "Don't shoot me Rosie, I am a social experiment, nothing more!"

Through the dark fog which was seeping through my brain, I sensed a movement between the two young women, Rosie passing the pistol over to Alice….

"It's not my fault! Please!"

The dark shape against my eyelids grew into the shape of a dish. If only we could all be wiser at the time, I thought. As I drew the dish towards me, as I saw it at my feet and as I stepped through, I thought I heard a loud explosion and then another, echoing down the tunnel, the sound of two pistol shots in the enclosed space.

33

Monks Bay, Isle of Wight. Nowadays.

My clothes were still wet. I was still in the same
chamber. It was pitch black. I reached into my pocket and
pulled out the torch, alarmed at how weak the beam was.
I could barely see. Rosie, Alice and the old man had gone.
So had the lantern. So had Nathan.

In the corner of the chamber were two things. One
was the chest and the other was a skeleton, the remains of
a black floppy tarpaulin hat perched on its head, the
bones of its legs ending in large boots. Gingerly, I
dragged myself up and got to my feet and approached the
chest, carefully skirting round the edge of the skeleton. I
stumbled across a pile of light round hardened balls
packed in what looked like grease paper, like old pork
pies. I kicked them away as I reached the chest. The lid
was surprisingly easy to lift and even in the weak light of
the torch, I could see the dull gleam of heavily tarnished
silver coins nearly up to the rim. On top of the coins was
an oblong piece of cardboard and a small leather-bound
book. I picked them both up and held the piece of
cardboard up in the torchlight, but the torch went out
suddenly as the battery finally died.

I began to shiver hard, my whole body racked with
shivering, and stumbled down the tunnel and reached the
end. I could just make out the form of the rusting iron
grill. I heaved all of my weight hard against it but it didn't
move. I put my fingers through the grill and felt along the
edge of the other side. I felt the top of a bolt driven into

the stone. It must have been put in in the last one hundred and fifty years. I was stuck. My shivering got so bad that I was barely able to stand up. I stood there shaking with cold and clasped my arms around my chest to preserve any heat that might be left. I got my hands through the grill and felt the other side for the bolt head. Tears of misery clogged my eyes as I felt for the bolt-head again. It had gone, snapped off. I pushed at the rusting iron grill and got it a few inches open, and then managed to squeeze through.

A bar of daylight showed under the door of the cellar and I stepped carefully over the accumulated rubbish of one hundred and fifty years to reach the door. I paused before I pulled it open. Then I did.

I walked through Luke's hall and into the kitchen. It was empty. But, thank God, it was warm. Luke's cardigan hung over the back of a chair. I sat down, and gazed out of the window. The clock showed that it was just after midnight. No time had passed at all.

34

Too tired and cold to move or think, I wrapped Luke's cardigan round my shoulders and filled the kettle, searching for tea bags, taking a carton of milk from the fridge. As the kettle boiled, I looked down at the oblong piece of cardboard I had found with the silver. It was folded. Printed in elegant curving letters on the front were the words, "Timothy Stevenson, Photographer" and an address. At the bottom was printed, "NEGATIVES KEPT, copies may be had at any time."

Fingers shaking, I opened it out and saw inside an old photograph mounted in one of the thick cardboard leaves, its corners stuck in slits. It was a picture of a group of children standing in rows, one above the other, gray colours blurred and darkened with age. Right in the centre of one of the lower rows, taller than her immediate neighbours, the face of a pretty girl stood out, staring defiantly right into the lens of the camera. She was wearing a white smock with a large smear covering the sleeve. Amazingly, you could see the title embossed on the book she held pressed to her chest. It was "Readings For Every Day In Lent".

I lifted the small book, turned the cover so I could read the title. *"The Magic of the Undercliff" A Volume of Songs and Lyrical Poems by Rose Olivia Cotton."* I glanced at the foot of the title page, "London 1850".

Eyes bleary, I flipped the leaves of the book and tried to focus. A page fell open, as if read many times over. I began to read.

Valediction for Adam
Remembrance fading as an ember fades;
Aching heart is all that remains,
I listen in the shadows and the shades,
Your voice and face to capture,
And hold them close to me.
The moon burns my mind when I stare,
at the brilliance I see there
resting at the water's rim, tarnished as my memory holds you
dim,
fades as silver as I try
to hold your memory close to me.
You say it was a witch who brought you here,
stepping into the moondish through a bowl on the sea's rim fire,
down the track upon the sea.
If so I thank the witch who brought you to me,
out of nowhere,
from the dark sky's churn;
but I thank not she
who took you from me,
never to return.

So there it was. A bubble of realisation formed and rose in my brain. The secret. Adam had been back before me. That was it. The undercurrent of his story. Luke had been right. It was a love sickness which he could never have explained. A loss in his heart that could never heal. The Witch's curse, carried down the generations from the original loss of that poor wretched Chinese woman. He had tried to tell us, but nobody could possibly have understood or believed him.

The understanding strengthened me. My brain fired up, overcoming my physical exhaustion, even my hunger. I had succeeded in my job, an incredible feeling of new pride filled me. And now, triumphant, generous, unselfish, I could give this to Luke and watch her face shine.

But no. I had to keep it all quiet. I would send my report to Driscoll, for what it was worth, but then I would help Adam. Really help him. I could really make a difference, for the first time in my life. I had nothing to lose. I had everything to give. I wasn't going to sit around waiting for the doorbell to ring. I found some chocolate biscuits and ate them all, drinking the best cup of tea I had ever tasted. I couldn't wait for Luke to wake up, my new warmth and self-esteem filling me, growing stronger, becoming a huge feeling of self-congratulation which lasted until the dawn.

"So. Jane."

I woke with a start. Lucretia Doe was standing in the kitchen doorway, considering me, the photograph, the book, sizing me up. Slowly. She was carrying a thick sheaf of dog-eared papers.

"Luke!" I blurted, "I have been waiting to tell you all night." I giggled, "I have cracked it! I've cracked the whole thing. Make a cuppa, sit down, and I'll tell you everything."

"Really?" She clearly hadn't slept well. Her eyes had no excitement, no sympathy, all kindness gone. Oddly, she looked much older, dried out, like she was at the end of a long struggle.

"I have something for you, something of yours." She laid the old papers on the table.

"So now you know we're not mad." Her mouth formed what looked uncomfortably like a smirk, "We can try to exorcise the ghosts, can't we?" She whispered, lifting her arm, waving her hand.

Suddenly, I noticed her finger nails. They were long. They were dirty.

She began scratching at the wooden door. Then spittle began seeping at the edge of her mouth. She coughed, her fingers pulling at her lips, her dark eyes staring at me.

The Luke I had known had gone. She was someone else, something, else.

She was beckoning. Beckoning to someone else through the door.

Adam came slowly through the doorway. Then another. My ex-patient. My ex-lover. Whom I had betrayed. Who had betrayed me. He looked thin. And angry. And satisfied.

"Now you can really help us all. Yes, you can really help us, Jane," She paused, "As you were supposed to all along."

The three of them nodded as they looked down at me, calmly distant, as a coven priestess and priests must look at a sacrificial lamb.

"After all, you never liked living in this time, did you Jane? You've never really liked living at all. Always dissatisfied, seeking an escape? Always running away?" A hint, just a suspicion, of kindness tinged her voice at last, "For whosoever will save her life shall lose it: but whosoever will lose her life for my sake, she shall save it."

"Well now you can escape forever. And Adam can find his life, his true love, become whole, for good or evil. Look upon it as an act of kindness. An act of kindness is an antidote to all the evil in this world."

She pushed the papers across the table. "Your story, Jane. Evidence of your insanity. Kept by us and copied out by Adam. Then photocopied by Driscoll. Written by you in the years after the wrecking in 1849, before you were committed as insane to Carisbrooke Lunatic Asylum. We'll be doing you a kindness when we send you back," She gave a small shrug, "This time forever."

"Why?" I looked at them in turn, begging, my mind fracturing, "Why me?"

"Alice Capper spent a very happy life after she married the ship's doctor." She paused, then spoke more slowly.

"Despite her scars, despite her wounds, his compassion on the voyage together turned into something much deeper. He loved her. They both survived the wrecking of the Sea Witch. After Alice shot her brother, knowing that they wouldn't be able to survive in Britain, they left together for New Zealand in the Spring of 1850. I believe they became farmers."

"So? So? So what the fuck has this got to do with me?" But I knew with a chill what was coming.

"The ship's doctor. His name was Tench. James Tench." Luke patted the pile of papers on the table, "The Cycle has indeed full turned. He was your ancestor." Luke turned to the others, "And so too was Alice Capper."

My ex was fiddling with a piece of rope.

"Alice's reprieve. You could call it an endowment."

She threw her last remark over her shoulder at me as she left me to the others.

"For the first time in your life, Jane. Kindness borne of sacrifice."

Epilogue

Isle of Wight County Press January 12th

Mystery Psychotherapist and Patient Still Missing

Concern grows as police confirm no progress at time of press with the search for fugitive Island psychotherapist Jane Tench and her troubled patient Adam Doe, after their disappearance at the time of the full moon before the Christmas holiday.

Island NHS Consultant Psychotherapist Driscoll has called for a full formal enquiry. Before her disappearance, Ms. Tench had mailed him a bulky dossier containing a highly questionable account of her dealings with Mr Doe, leading experts to question her own mental health. Mr. Driscoll added that it can be disclosed that Miss Tench had a history of inappropriate dealings with her patients.

Mr. Driscoll has promised every co-operation with the police, the NHS and other authorities to locate the whereabouts of Ms. Tench and Mr. Doe and to bring Ms. Tench to account for her actions.

Adam Doe's grandmother, Lucretia Doe, of the Cliff Path, Bonchurch, declined to comment, saying only that she was devastated by her loss.

The search continues.

Acknowledgement

The Author is deeply indebted to
the Ventnor & District Local History Society
and begs the forgiveness of its members for any historical
inaccuracies, pleading artistic licence.

Printed in Poland
by Amazon Fulfillment
Poland Sp. z o.o., Wrocław